# The Shluffmuffin Boy
# Is History

Don't miss the other spine-tingling
Secrets of Dripping Fang adventures!

SECRETS OF

DRIPPING FANG

BOOK ONE:
The Onts

BOOK TWO:
Treachery and Betrayal at Jolly Days

BOOK THREE:
The Vampire's Curse

BOOK FOUR:
Fall of the House of Mandible

# SECRETS OF
# DRIPPING FANG

## BOOK FIVE

## The Shluffmuffin Boy
## Is History

# DAN GREENBURG

### Illustrations by SCOTT M. FISCHER

HARCOURT, INC.

Orlando   Austin   New York   San Diego   Toronto   London

*I want to thank my editor, Allyn Johnston, for her macabre yet soulful*
*sense of humor, for her eagerness to explore ideas beyond the bounds of taste,*
*for understanding an author's poignant thirst for praise, and for helping*
*me say exactly what I'm trying to say, except more gooder.*
*I also want to thank Scott M. Fischer,*
*an artist with dizzying technical abilities and a demented genius*
*at combining terror and humor in the same illustration.*

—D. G.

Text copyright © 2006 by Dan Greenburg
Illustrations copyright © 2006 by Scott M. Fischer

Requests for permission to make copies of any part of the work
should be submitted online at www.harcourt.com/contact or mailed
to the following address: Permissions Department, Harcourt, Inc.,
6277 Sea Harbor Drive, Orlando, Florida 32887-6777.

www.HarcourtBooks.com

Library of Congress Cataloging-in-Publication Data
Greenburg, Dan.
Secrets of Dripping Fang. Book five, the Shluffmuffin boy is
history/Dan Greenburg; illustrations by Scott M. Fischer.—1st ed.
p. cm.
Summary: Although a paid assassin is stalking Wally while
his twin sister Cheyenne is under the power of the queen ont,
it is up to them, their vampire dad, and their friends to
save the human race from the giant onts.
[1. Twins—Fiction.  2. Ants—Fiction.  3. Vampires—Fiction.
4. Cincinnati (Ohio)—Fiction.]  I. Fischer, Scott M., ill.  II. Title.
III. Title: The Shluffmuffin boy is history.
PZ7.G8278Sef  2006
[Fic]    2006005865
ISBN-13: 978-0-15-206035-0  ISBN-10: 0-15-206035-9

Text set in Meridien
Designed by Linda Lockowitz

First edition
A C E G H F D B

# Contents

# The Shluffmuffin Boy Is History

# CHAPTER 1

# Bargaining for Cheyenne's Life

Cheyenne Shluffmuffin lay in bed, shivering. Although the girl's slim body quaked with cold, her thin pajamas and sheets were soaked in sweat. Her skin was so hot, it scalded the fingertips of whoever touched her.

The darkened room in the attic of the odd house in the forest smelled like cherry cough syrup, menthol, and stale bedclothes. The sound of her labored, wheezing breathing was hard to listen to.

The doctor removed a glass thermometer from between Cheyenne's parched lips and held it close to the bedside light.

"How high is my temperature, Doctor?" Cheyenne asked weakly.

"A hundred and six," he said.

A tortured cough momentarily convulsed her body.

"That's . . . not so high," she gasped when she could breathe again, "is it?"

"No," said the doctor, "not compared to the temperature of boiling water."

Wally, Cheyenne's ten-year-old twin brother, leaned close to Shirley Spydelle's ear. "Are doctors supposed to be sarcastic?" he whispered.

Shirley shook her head. "No, Wally," she whispered back. "But that's troll doctors for you—no bedside manner. However, they do make house calls." Shirley rubbed four of her eight legs through her silk pajamas and pulled her robe more tightly around herself. Even giant spiders sometimes feel a chill.

"Hey, honey, a hundred and six is *nothing*," said Vampire Dad, pulling the blankets up over his shivering daughter. "I once had a hundred and twenty." This was an outrageous lie to make

Cheyenne feel better and she knew it. Dad had never had a temperature higher than a hundred and four, and for the past three years he'd had no temperature at all.

The troll doctor yanked his stethoscope out of his long floppy ears and zipped up his medical bag. His wart-covered head was so large, it threatened to tip him over on his stubby legs and send him crashing to the floor.

Wally, Dad, Shirley, and Shirley's human husband, Edgar, followed the troll as he hopped down three flights of stairs to the front door.

"Okay, *amigos*," said the troll, "that'll be two hundred bucks. Cash."

Dad looked at Edgar, then shrugged and raised his palms.

"My word, Doctor," said Edgar in his charming British accent. "When we spoke on the phone, I understood you to say *one* hundred."

"Right," said the troll. "A hundred for the house call, a hundred for the stairs. Stairs are murder on a troll's legs. If I'd known you had stairs, I never would've come."

4

Edgar pulled a roll of twenties, as old and limp as cloth, from his wallet. He counted out a sheaf of them and extended it to the troll, who snatched it quick as a toad's tongue.

"What is your prognosis, Doctor?" asked Edgar. He struck a wooden match with his thumbnail, held the flame close to the bowl of his pipe, and inhaled deeply. It failed to light.

"Well, Professor," said the troll, "there's a very good chance she'll live through the night, in which case I wouldn't be surprised if she makes it all the way to lunch tomorrow."

"And after that?" Wally asked.

"After that?" said the troll. "After that your guess is as good as mine. To be on the safe side, though, I'd probably have me a good funeral home standing by."

The troll opened the front door. "Heigh-ho," he said, and then hopped through the door and went down the walk, swinging his black bag.

Wally, Edgar, Shirley, and Vampire Dad stared out the door after him, paralyzed by his dark news, until Edgar realized that leaving doors open at night in Dripping Fang Forest was unwise, and promptly slammed it shut.

"That guy may be a doctor, but he's a total creep," said Wally. "And I'm sorry, I know you're not supposed to notice trolls' heads and legs and warts and stuff, but—"

"Wally, the fact that he's a troll has nothing to do with his being a creep," Dad interrupted. "He'd be just as creepy if he were human. And I refuse to believe that Cheyenne's chances are as bad as he said. A high fever is a *good* sign. A high fever shows that the body is fighting the infection. Isn't that right, Professor?"

"Quite," said Edgar, sucking in vain on his unlit pipe. "The fever is nothing to worry about. It's the coughing up of blood that *I* don't like. Now, I'm not a doctor, but I do think she's going to be just fine."

"So do I," said Vampire Dad, trying hard not to think about all that luscious blood going to waste. "The important thing is to make sure she drinks plenty of liquids. Then she'll be fine."

"She'll absolutely be fine," said Wally.

*She's going to die*, said Wally silently. *My poor twin sister is going to die. Oh, God, please don't let her die. Please, please don't let her die. If you let her live, I'll do anything you want, anything. I'll become a better boy, a better brother. I'll . . . I'll try to be more positive. Cheyenne has always wanted me to be more positive. If she pulls through this, I'll become a total optimist, I swear, even more than Cheyenne. Much more. If you let Cheyenne live, I'll be such an optimist, I'll make her look like* me *by comparison!*

"She may seem bad now," said Dad, "but it's always darkest before the dawn. By morning she'll be fever free."

*If it seems certain that she's dying*, Dad wondered, *can I bite her on the neck just before she utters her last gasp, before her heart contracts that final time and squeezes out her last pulse of nourishing blood, and then have her join me as a member of the living dead? No! I cannot even think such thoughts! I cannot let her die! I don't know if I can believe in a God who let me drown in a Porta Potti and become a vampire, but I'm willing to keep an open mind. Okay, God, if you do exist, and if you let her live, I'll do anything*

*you want me to. I'll give up forever my infernal thirst
for human blood. I'll get over how hurt I am that she
and Wally prefer to have the Spydelles be their parents
instead of me. If you let her live, I'll tell them I won't
even stand in the way of the Spydelles legally adopting
my children.*

"She'll be fit as a fiddle by morning," said
Edgar.

*What can I promise you, Lord, to convince you to
spare this child's life?* Edgar prayed. *I know—if she
lives, I shall tell Vampire Dad he no longer has to
sleep in the garage at night; he can come back and
sleep in the house. Sure, our lives will no longer be
safe from his horrid bloodlust, but I'm willing to
make that sacrifice if you will only let this poor child
live.*

"The important thing," said Shirley, "is to put
ice packs on her and get the fever down. That's
what's going to do the trick. She'll be fine by
morning, you mark my words."

*Here's what I'm prepared to do if Cheyenne's life
is spared,* thought Shirley. *If Cheyenne lives, I'll give
up my desire to have babies of my own, and I'll insist*

*that the twins return to their real father, bloodsucking demon or not.*

The phone rang. Shirley picked it up in the living room. "Hello?"

"Shirl?" said a breathless female voice. "It's Hortense Jolly, at the Jolly Days Orphanage. We're worried *sick* about poor little Cheyenne. How's she doing? Still alive?"

"Yes, Hortense, she's still alive," said Shirley, rolling all eight of her eyes. "What can I do for you?"

"The orphans here at Jolly Days and I are holding an all-night candlelight vigil for her," said Hortense. "And I've written a song especially for the occasion, which they'd like to sing her. Is this a good time?"

"No," said Shirley, "couldn't be a worse one."

"Good," said Hortense, "it'll only take a minute. Could you just hold the receiver up to her ear?"

"No, Hortense. Cheyenne is in the attic. There's no phone up there, and I'm three flights down in the living room."

"Oh, then could you holler up to her to come downstairs and listen to this? I really think she'll get a kick out of it."

"Cheyenne is running a very high fever," said Shirley with exaggerated slowness. "I'm not having her get out of bed to listen to a *song*."

"Okay, Shirl, whatever," said Hortense. "Here comes the song. Ready, Orphans? A-one, a-two, a-three, and . . ."

*Hi, we heard that you are sick and at death's door.*
*Your fever's high, you're coughing blood, your*
 *joints are sore.*
*You must rally your defenses—*
*Don't take leave of all your senses—*
*If you die, we cannot see you anymore.*

*What you have is just the flu, a simple virus,*
*Which is better than the plague, though not*
 *desirous.*
*Take two aspirin, rest in bed;*
*Drink those fluids, don't get dead.*
*If these tips don't make you better, you can fire us.*

"Thank you, Orphans!" called Hortense. "So that's the song, Shirl," said Hortense into the phone. "Try and remember all the lyrics when you sing it back to her. Which reminds me, I hear you and Professor Spydelle have adopted Cheyenne and Wally without consulting me. This may not be the best time to mention it, but the twins are actually *my* orphans, and when anybody adopts my orphans, I get an adoption fee of six hundred dollars per. I do hope you can put a check for twelve hundred into the mail to no later than tomorrow. Now, I know Cheyenne is really sick, so, needless to say, if you send the twelve hundred and she were to, you know, *pass on* . . . Well, of course I'd refund six hundred of that, no questions asked—that's just the kind of woman I am."

In the background, Shirley heard children shout out questions.

"Oh, Shirl, the orphans want to know: If Cheyenne *does* pass on, could they have her clothes?"

Shirley hung up the phone.

# CHAPTER 2

# Bring Me the Head of Wally Shluffmuffin—and, If There's Time, Maybe a Foot

"Tell us everything you know about the beasts who burned down the House of Mandible, murdered Dagmar, incinerated the babies, and disfigured you so horribly," demanded the whale-sized creature reclining on the ninety-foot sofa.

The gigantic Ont Queen was clad in canvas camouflage fatigues that had been pieced together from several army tents. Jammed between her huge mandibles was the stub of a large cigar that had gone out.

The royal sofa stood in the middle of an immense cavern with a high domelike ceiling.

Stalactites hung from the ceiling like teeth from a gargantuan dinosaur's mouth. Cannon-sized stalagmites sprouted from the floor. Tall wrought-iron candelabra held a thousand lit candles. The cavern itself was entirely plated in twenty-four-carat gold. Even the stalactites and stalagmites were plated in gold, which reflected the flames of the flickering candles.

The queen was speaking to Hedy Mandible, a six-foot-tall Ont who wore a partial mask covering one side of her disfigured face.

"My Queen," replied Hedy, "it all happened so fast, and there was so much confusion, I can't be sure. I remember seeing Cheyenne and Wally Shluffmuffin, of course. I remember seeing a skinny man with a pipe, a tall woman, and thirty or forty filthy children who stank like barn animals. I know there was an enormous spider. I know there was a man with wings and fangs, who may have been a vampire."

"They shall all die appropriately horrid deaths," said the queen. "An eye for an eye, a tooth for a tooth, a mandible for a mandible."

"All but Cheyenne, of course," said Hedy. "I feel she can be quite valuable to us. She's unusually positive and open to suggestion. I know I can train her to be an effective ambassador for our cause."

The queen laughed nastily. "To convince the human fools they have nothing to fear from us, so they'll be utterly unprepared for our invasion when it comes. Excellent! You say she has already been neutralized?"

"My Queen, I put her under a strong posthypnotic suggestion," said Hedy. "Cheyenne is now our slave. While Cheyenne was in a trance, Dagmar and I took her to downtown Cincinnati to spray flu virus on crowds of humans. Even as we speak, worker onts are circulating in the city, collecting snot-filled tissues from humans with flu to feed the hungry larvae in our nurseries. All I have to do is speak a particular triggering phrase to Cheyenne and she'll do whatever I tell her."

"All the more reason to kill this Wally person," said the queen. "He is her twin brother, is he not? They are very close?"

"Extremely close, My Queen."

"We understand human twins often develop a secret language, known only to them," said the queen. "Some can communicate by ESP. So this boy could be a dangerous influence on Cheyenne, especially since you tell us he's so negative."

"My Queen, the boy is as negative as the girl is positive," said Hedy.

A worker ont in denim overalls approached the queen's sofa, knelt, and whispered something. Without glancing at her, the queen waved her away like a mosquito. Humiliated, the worker ont withdrew.

"Now, how do we kill this vampire?" asked the queen. "How do you kill someone who is already dead?"

"Well, the traditional methods," said Hedy, "are a wooden stake through the heart or—"

"—a silver bullet," said the queen impatiently. "Yes, yes, we know. But our first victim must be Wally Shluffmuffin, because he was the ringleader of the attack on Mandible House."

"Right, Your Highness," said Hedy.

"Then we shall send over a platoon of our girls," said the queen. "A platoon of army onts will terminate the Shluffmuffin boy in an instant. He will be history."

"But Your Highness," said Hedy, "the giant spider and the vampire will certainly come to his defense. Your girls are very effective in traditional warfare, but frankly, we don't know how they'd do against either a giant spider or a vampire. Meaning no disrespect, I think I have a better plan. I suggest we hire a professional assassin who's used to nontraditional hits."

"Do you have such an individual in mind?"

"I do, My Queen," said Hedy. "They call him The Jackal."

"The Jackal," said the queen. She removed the dead cigar stub from between her mandibles and handed it to a worker ont. "We think we saw a movie about him."

"No, no, My Queen, that was a fictional human whose *name* was The Jackal. This is a

18

real jackal. He's a professional assassin. He has never failed."

"Send for him," said the queen. "We shall determine whether or not he is the one we can trust to kill Wally Shluffmuffin."

CHAPTER 3

# Wiggle Room

It was long after midnight in the attic room that smelled of cherry cough syrup, menthol, and stale sheets. Edgar, Wally, and Dad had been taking turns applying ice packs to the trembling feverish girl. Cheyenne's skin was yellow, waxy, and lifeless. She swam in sweat, but shuddered as if she were drowning in the Arctic Ocean.

"I'm s-s-so c-c-cold," Cheyenne whispered. "I m-m-mean it's r-r-*refreshing,* b-b-but c-c-cold."

"I'm so sorry you're cold, honey," said Dad. "But we really have to get your temperature down."

"I th-th-thought you s-s-said my f-f-fever was a g-g-*good* s-s-sign."

"Well, it *is* a good sign, honey," said Dad. "A *very* good sign. But we still don't want it to go too high, is all."

"H-h-how h-h-high is t-t-*too* high?"

"Oh, I don't know," said Dad. "Anything over, um, a hundred and twenty."

The little girl sneezed loudly and clutched her father's arm. "I'm n-n-not g-g-going to d-d-die, am I, D-d-daddy?" she whispered.

Dad shook his head so violently, the room swung back and forth before him in blurry arcs.

"Of *course* you're not, sweetheart!" he said, tears welling in his eyes and spilling down his cheeks. "It's just a little flu."

Dad helped Cheyenne blow her nose into a tissue, as Shirley delicately picked tiny shards of glass and beads of mercury from every crease and crevice in Cheyenne's bedclothes. The last time Edgar had tried to take Cheyenne's temperature, the heat of her mouth had shattered the thermometer.

*Please let her live*, prayed Wally, Dad, Edgar, and Shirley. They silently restated their various

21

vows—to become optimistic, to be selfless about the twins' adoption, and to give up the desire to drink human blood.

Cheyenne slid into a delirious feverish sleep, a crazed cartoon of whirling monsters, cackling demons, and out-of-control chords from a massive pipe organ. Then, exhausted by the hour and by the effort of trying to lower Cheyenne's fever with ice packs, one by one Dad, Shirley, Edgar, and Wally fell asleep as well.

As the black sky bleached slowly into pale blue and the bluish pink of morning, they were awakened by a voice. "Hey, guys, it sure is warm in here. You mind if I open a window?"

It was Cheyenne. Sitting up in bed! Her hair was soaking wet, but her eyes were bright and the color of her skin was that of a living girl.

Dad reached forward and felt her forehead. "You're not hot anymore, honey," he said. "Your fever must have broken."

"You did it, Cheyenne!" shouted Wally. "Way to break a fever! Yee-*ha*!" He gave her a high five that nearly knocked her out of bed.

"Oh, Cheyenne, dear, I'm so grateful!" said Shirley, wrapping her in several longish arms.

"Congratulations, my dear," said Edgar, shaking Cheyenne's hand. "I believe the worst is now over."

They all took turns hugging her.

Then there was a moment of awkward silence as everybody realized they were now stuck keeping the bargains they'd made if Cheyenne survived.

*Oh, man*, thought Wally. *I promised to stop being negative if she lived. How can I ever do that? I haven't had a positive thought in weeks.*

*Oh, bother*, thought Edgar. *Now I have to tell Dad that the twins don't really prefer me as a father, that they were just pretending in order to save my life. So now we'll lose the twins and Shirley will demand to have children of our own, and then she'll eat me. This is awkward.*

*Thank you, God*, Dad prayed. *I guess I pretty much have to believe in you now. But listen, how literally do I have to live up to my promises? I mean, do I really have to tell the Spydelles I approve of their adopting my children? And am I now supposed to totally lose my taste for blood, or is there maybe a little wiggle room here? I mean, all right, I'll never drink another* glass *of human blood. But would it be okay to do lesser things? Like, say, collect tissues from Edgar's daily shaving cuts and make from them a weak soup?*

Early that same morning on the streets of downtown Cincinnati, the tops of the tallest buildings caught the sun, making the glare on the windows too bright to look at. Still groggy with sleep, office workers made their way down the streets toward the towers of stone and glass in which they toiled. Some carried cardboard containers of fragrant, steaming coffee, some carried newspapers folded under their arms, but all clutched Kleenexes and regularly sneezed and snorted into them.

They scarcely noticed the ladies in the wide-brimmed black hats, black sunglasses, black gloves and capes, who, like grim Santas, stood on every corner with burlap sacks at their feet. Each time a passing worker sneezed, a black-hatted lady said "Gesundheit!" and swiftly snatched the tissue out of the startled person's hand, then stuffed it into her sack. Most people assumed these were oddly uniformed city sanitation workers and were grateful for the service. If they'd known the intended destination of their phlegmy tissues, they might not have been so pleased.

# CHAPTER 4

# Biting the Bullet

*M*r. *Shluffmuffin, I wish to inform you . . . No,* no, no, not so bloody formal. And don't call him Mr. Shluffmuffin, for pity's sake, call him Sheldon. *Sheldon, Shirley and I just wanted to tell you that the twins . . . Hmmm, how to phrase it gracefully? Oh my word, here he comes!*

"I say, Sheldon," Edgar sang out with forced cheerfulness, "good morning, sir! Sheldon, Shirley and I just wanted to tell you that the twins—"

"Professor," Dad blurted, "I've-thought-it-over-and-much-as-I-hate-to-admit-this-the-twins-will-be-better-off-with-you-and-Shirley-as-parents-than-they-would-with-me-so-I-hereby-give-you-my-permission-to-adopt-them-congratulations."

Edgar stared at Dad, dumbfounded. "Excuse me?" he said, not sure he'd heard what he'd just heard.

Dad drew a deep breath and began again. "I said, I've thought it over and, much as I hate to admit this, the twins will be better off with you and Shirley as parents than they would with me, so I hereby give you my permission to adopt them. Congratulations."

Edgar was speechless. *Great Caesar's ghost,* he thought, *what must one do here? Proceed to tell him what I was going to say, regardless? If I do, he'll retract his offer and, in all likelihood, accept mine. Then Shirley will insist upon having babies, and I shall end up dead. If I say nothing, I can continue to live and I can adopt the twins, but I shall dishonor my pledge and know that I'm a complete scoundrel.*

"Professor," said Dad, frowning, "did you hear me?"

"Did I hear you?" Edgar repeated, "Yes, yes, of course I heard you."

"Somehow I thought you'd have more of a reaction than this."

*If you're going to do the honorable thing*, Edgar told himself, *this would be the moment.* "A reaction?" he said. "Well, Sheldon, my reaction is that I'm . . . speechless. Overwhelmed. Overwhelmed by your generosity, sir. I thank you so much for such a generous gesture." *And I myself am a shameless, spineless, cowardly scoundrel.*

"I'm sorry if I interrupted you," said Dad. "What was it you were going to say before I spoke?"

"What was I going to say to you?"

"Yes," said Dad.

"Um, you know, I haven't the foggiest," said Edgar. *Shameless, spineless, sniveling, simpering scoundrel. Loathsome, lily-livered, chickenhearted, toad-licking, utterly reprehensible scoundrel.*

Dad walked into Cheyenne and Wally's ground-floor bedroom, where Cheyenne had moved after her fever broke. She was sitting up in bed, talking to Wally and drinking hot cocoa with marshmallows that Shirley had brought her. Weak sun from an overcast sky leaked through the bedroom window.

"Morning, Dad," said Cheyenne, sneezing and blowing her nose.

"Morning, Dad," said Wally.

"Morning, kids," said Dad. "I'm so glad you're better, honey. I was just telling Edgar about an important decision I've come to: I decided I no longer mind your being adopted by the Spydelles. In fact, I think it might be the best solution for all of us."

Cheyenne's eyes filled with instant tears, but Wally held his back by a supreme act of will.

"I mean, that's what you kids seemed to want," said Dad with a forced smile. "I thought you'd be pleased. Are you?"

"Yeah, Dad, sure," said Wally. "I'm pleased."

"Well, good. I'm glad." Dad turned to Cheyenne. "What about you, hon?"

Cheyenne urged her face into what she hoped

was a smile but looked more like a grimace. "If that's what you'd prefer, I'm pleased, too, Dad," she said, wiping her eyes and nose.

"Well, fine," said Dad. There was an awkward pause during which everyone looked everywhere in the room except at one another. "Well, okay then," he said, and left.

"How could Dad even *say* such a thing?" asked Cheyenne when she and Wally were alone again. "I thought he loved us."

"Yeah, I thought so, too," said Wally. Then he remembered his vow to be positive. "Look, Cheyenne, we still have each other, okay? We don't need anyone else. Dad still loves us, but becoming a vampire and all has probably screwed up his fatherly feelings. It's the best he can do for now. Probably it'll get better, but in the meantime we need to understand that and love him the way he is."

"I guess you're right," she said. She blew her nose loudly into a Kleenex.

The phone rang. Wally picked up the receiver.

"Spydelle residence," he said.

"Oh, Wally, is that you?" asked Hortense. "I'm just calling to find out about poor Cheyenne. Is she . . . still in our midst, or did she pass on during the night?"

"Cheyenne is fine," said Wally. "Thanks for asking. The fever broke late last night, and she's almost back to normal."

31

"Really?" said Hortense. "Oh, I'm so happy. You don't know how happy I am. Children," she called, "Cheyenne didn't die after all! What? Well, I don't think so, but I'll ask. Wally, one of the orphans wants to know if he could at least have her socks."

Wally started to hang up the phone, then remembered his promise. He took a deep breath and controlled his anger. "Cheyenne still needs both pairs of hers," he said. "But I'll look around and see if I have an extra pair of mine I could spare. Have a wonderful day."

# CHAPTER 5

# An Audience with the Queen

Cheyenne slept fitfully, her dreams filled with disturbing images—grotesque people with mutilated faces peered through the windows of her bedroom, smooshing their noses and mouths against the glass, tapping to get in. She awoke to the sound of tapping.

She tried to clear her head, but strands of the dream still clung to her like cobwebs. She could still hear the tapping. She gasped as she realized that there really *was* somebody outside the bedroom, a dark shape tapping at the window.

Now the dark shape held something up to the glass, a huge white cardboard sign, printed with thick letters: WOULD YOU LIKE TO MEET THE

BABIES, DEAR? The sign was removed, and the dark shape melted back into the depths of the forest.

Cheyenne had no idea what the sign meant, yet at some deep level of consciousness it made sense to her. Unaware that Wally was awake, she slowly turned and walked zombielike out of the house in her pajamas. Curious and suspicious, Wally crept out of bed, pulled on a sweater, and followed her.

The forest was thick with soft, moist fog. Walking through it was like wading through snowdrifts over one's head, snowdrifts of tiny feathers. Shortly after Cheyenne wandered into the fog, the dark shape materialized beside her, taking her by the hand and guiding her away. To follow them without being noticed, Wally had to stay close behind as they faded in and out of focus in the clouds of cottony mist.

Wally knew there were packs of man-eating wolves in the forest and giant slugs that dined on orphans' feet, but he couldn't afford to worry

about that now. If they wanted to attack him, then attack him is what they would do. At one point he sensed that he, too, was being followed, and he thought he heard someone whisper, "We could sink our teeth into your throat whenever we like," but it might not even have been a voice—it might merely have been the sound of the wind sighing through the trees. If it *had* been the wind sighing through the trees, though, that wouldn't explain the hot breath he'd felt on the back of his neck.

Wally had seen the sign pressed up against the window, too, and it made even less sense to him than to his sister. THE BABIES was probably a reference to the giant ont larvae, but hadn't all of those been cremated in the fire at Mandible House? And if Dagmar and Hedy had died in the fire as well, then who had held up the sign and who was guiding Cheyenne now? More important, where was she being taken?

When Cheyenne and her escort had been walking for at least twenty minutes, they slowed down. Abruptly, two figures appeared out of the fog, huge female onts in green berets and camouflage fatigues.

"State your name and the nature of your business," snapped one of them.

"Cheyenne Shluffmuffin would like to see the babies," said her escort.

"The Ont Queen is expecting her," replied the ont who'd spoken.

Cheyenne's escort took her into what appeared to be the mouth of a cave, then they both vanished.

*The Ont Queen is expecting you?* Wally was astonished to hear there was such a thing as an ont queen. He had thought all the onts had been killed in the battle at Mandible House. He was sickened at Cheyenne's apparent disloyalty to the human race. Then, remembering his vow, he forced himself to see the situation in an optimistic light: *Maybe this isn't as bad as it looks. Yeah, maybe Cheyenne isn't being disloyal to humans after all. Maybe she's actually a double agent, spying on onts for us humans. Or maybe she's just researching an extra-credit science project. Or something.*

The two army onts were clearly guarding the cave. All Wally could do was wait for Cheyenne to reappear.

Cheyenne was escorted downward through a maze of subterranean tunnels. One of these opened onto an astonishing gold cave with a very high ceiling and numerous candles.

The Ont Queen reclined on her ninety-foot royal sofa. She was surrounded by at least forty worker and army onts. There was a damp coppery smell in the air.

"Hello, dear," said a familiar voice behind Cheyenne.

Cheyenne turned and saw Hedy, the half mask partially covering her face.

"Hedy," said Cheyenne. "But I thought you were . . ."

"Dead? Burned to a crisp? Only partly," said Hedy. "Poor Dagmar is no more, but I survived, horribly disfigured, to carry on our great work. I'm happy to see you again, dear."

"Hedy, kindly introduce our guest," demanded the Ont Queen.

"Yes, Your Highness," said Hedy. "This is Cheyenne Shluffmuffin, a human, but one who is sympathetic to our cause. Cheyenne, this is the Mother of All Mothers, the Queen of the Onts of Ohio. You may address her as Your Highness or My Queen."

"Hi, Your Highness," said Cheyenne, sneezing, blowing her nose, and looking around. "You have a nice place here."

"Does its size surprise you, Cheyenne?"

"Yes, Your Highness."

The queen opened a claw and held it out at her side. A worker ont swiftly placed a drink into it.

"Besides this one in suburban Cincinnati," said the Ont Queen, sipping her drink, "we have colonies throughout Ohio—underneath Cleveland, Columbus, Canton, Dayton, Youngstown,

Akron, Toledo, Ashtabula, and Upper Sandusky. We also have moles scattered all over nearby states—Kentucky, Indiana, and West Virginia."

"Moles?" said Cheyenne. "Do you mean human spies, or onts in disguise?"

"*Moles,*" said the queen. "Small furry animals, with pointed snouts, that burrow underground and happen to be sympathetic to our cause and that do not attack us." Her voice suddenly turned angry and shook with emotion. "We are enraged by the attack on Mandible House and the death of Dagmar and the larvae! We shall avenge this atrocity and bring ont justice swiftly to all the perpetrators!"

"The fire was an accident, Your Highness," said Cheyenne, wiping her nose. "Nobody wanted anybody to die. They were just trying to rescue me."

"This was no accident, this was a carefully orchestrated surprise attack by a well-trained commando team!" shouted the queen. "Tell us, who besides the attack force knows about the Onts?"

"No one else, Your Highness," said Cheyenne. "Nobody believed me and Wally when we told them about Dagmar and Hedy—that they were breeding super-larvae and planning to replace mankind and end life on Earth as we know it. Everyone *I* know saw Dagmar, Hedy, and all the babies die in the fire."

"Cheyenne, dear," said Hedy, "you are going to be quite valuable to us. We onts count on you to come to this cave whenever we summon you and feed us information on those responsible for the deaths of Dagmar and the babies."

"Okay," said Cheyenne, "as long as you don't ask me to be disloyal to my family or friends."

The Ont Queen glared at Hedy, shook her head, and rolled her eyes. "We understood this was to be her first training session," said the queen. "This is a disappointing start."

"Then let me put her into a deeper trance, My Queen," said Hedy. "Cheyenne, dear, I want you to listen to the sound of my voice. I want you to imagine that, as I speak, your body is filling up with lovely warm liquid. Lovely warm liquid spreading from the tips of your toes right up to the top of your head."

*If she's trying to hypnotize me, it won't work,* Cheyenne thought, her mind rapidly clouding up. *You can't hypnotize someone if they don't want to be hypnotized, can you?*

"Are you imagining the lovely warm liquid filling up your body from your toes to your head?" Hedy asked.

"Yes, Ont Hedy," Cheyenne mumbled, and slumped to the floor.

By the time Cheyenne reappeared at the mouth of the cave, Wally figured that at least an hour had passed. She seemed a little wobbly. The escort said something he couldn't hear to the guards, then guided her back into the forest.

The fog had begun to lift. A bright moon was trying to poke through the mist, making it glow mysteriously. A light wind hummed through the bushes, carrying faint whiffs of pine and cedar. As he followed Cheyenne and the escort this time, Wally had to keep farther back so he wouldn't be noticed. Because there was now greater visibility, he was able to recognize certain landmarks.

The dark shape escorted Cheyenne almost to the door of the Spydelles' house, then vanished in the mist. Cheyenne seemed dazed.

Wally stepped forward, put his arms around her, and held her tight. "Thank heaven you're safe!" he said.

"Huh?" said Cheyenne. She didn't seem to recognize him.

"What were you doing visiting the Ont Queen?" he asked.

"Visiting the *what*?"

"The Ont Queen."

"What's an ont queen?" she said, then seemed to come out of her daze. "Hey, what are we doing outside?" She sneezed. "And why am I in my pj's?"

"You really don't know?"

She shook her head.

"Honest?" said Wally. "You swear?"

"Honest, I swear. Tell me."

"Okay," said Wally. "But first, let's get inside where it's safe."

He took her into the house, not turning on lights for fear of waking the Spydelles, bumping into several pieces of furniture in the dark. As soon as they were safely back in their bedroom, he began to speak again.

"About two hours ago we were both in bed," he said. "There was a tapping at the window there." He pointed to the window. "You woke up. I was already awake. There was somebody outside the window. Holding up a sign."

"A sign?" said Cheyenne. "What kind of a sign?"

"I couldn't read the whole thing," said Wally. "But it said something about meeting the babies. You left the house. Whoever held up the sign was waiting for you. They led you off through the forest, and I followed."

"You followed me *where*?"

"To a big cave," said Wally. "Two guards asked who you were and what your business was. Whoever took you there said your name. They

44

said you wanted to see the babies. The soldiers said the Ont Queen was expecting you. Then the person who brought you took you into the cave. You were gone about an hour. Do you remember what you did in there?"

Cheyenne shook her head.

"You think maybe they did something to make you forget? Like when extraterrestrials abduct humans? Like when they examine them in their UFOs? You think they hypnotized you or something?"

Cheyenne shook her head and wiped her nose. "Nobody can make you do anything under hypnosis that you wouldn't do when you're awake," she said. "I read that somewhere."

"That's a myth," said Wally. "I read more than you. Anybody can make anybody do anything they like. And the worse a thing it is, the easier it is." He sighed and shook his head. "Okay, I shouldn't have said that. I'm not talking that way anymore."

"You're not talking *what* way anymore?" said Cheyenne.

"Negatively."

"You're not?" she said. "How come?"

"Cheyenne, you were pretty sick the other night," he said. "I was afraid you weren't going to make it. I did a lot of thinking. I made a deal with God or somebody. I said that if you lived, I'd give up being so negative. I said I'd become an optimist."

"You really said that?"

Wally nodded.

"Oh, Wally, that's just so cool," she said. "That's about the nicest thing I've ever heard you say." She hugged him.

# CHAPTER 6

# Enter The Jackal

Emerging from the terminal at Northern Kentucky International Airport, the stranger felt pleased with himself. Following the terse call from a woman named Hedy Mandible, which he'd received in an outdoor phone booth on a street in Akron—a conversation in which the only words he'd spoken were "Yes," "No," and "Operator, the *other* party is paying for the call"—he spent several hours researching giant ants on the Internet. Then he'd flown to Cincinnati.

He hailed a taxi outside the terminal, got into the cab, and gave the driver the address of a newsstand in downtown Cincinnati.

When the cab arrived at his destination, the stranger got out across the street from the newsstand where the Mandible woman had suggested they meet. Apart from the elderly man wearing a Cincinnati Reds ball cap who seemed to be in charge, there was only one other person at the newsstand—a tall woman wearing a wide-brimmed black hat, black sunglasses, a long black cape, and full-length black gloves. The stranger walked up and down the block twice. Satisfied that he'd seen nothing suspicious, he crossed the street.

The tall woman was, as she had been instructed, reading a copy of *Boys' Life*. Picking up another copy of *Boys' Life*, the stranger leafed through it. Then, without looking at her, he said, "It was in this publication that I learned how to start a fire using only a magnifying glass to focus the sun's rays. Except at night and on cloudy days, I no longer have any use for matches."

"I detest matches," said the tall woman, without looking at the stranger.

"You folks planning to buy those magazines or what?" said the old man in the Reds ball cap.

The stranger looked quickly at the old man. He was only the proprietor, not a threat. "We're trying to decide," he said, turning back to his magazine.

"Are you the one who calls himself The Jackal?" asked the woman quietly, without looking at him.

"And if I am?" said the stranger.

"That's not too original a name, dear," said the woman. "I've seen at least two different movies with an assassin who called himself that."

"Several years ago," said the stranger in a lower voice, "there was a man who called himself The Jackal. He was an impostor, a human. I, on the other hand, am the genuine article." He removed a black leather glove and examined the claws of his right front paw. "You have called me here because you need to have somebody disposed of and you've heard that I'm the best. Who is the target?"

"A boy named Wally Shluffmuffin," said the

tall woman. "He lives in Dripping Fang Forest, on the outskirts of Cincinnati."

"What makes this boy so dangerous that you must hire a professional assassin to terminate him?" asked the stranger.

"He led an attack team that included an enormous spider, a vampire, and a gang of evil orphans. They killed my sister and hundreds of innocent babies."

"If you ain't buyin' those magazines," said the old man, "put 'em back. This ain't no public library."

"We're still *deciding*," said the stranger. He turned back to his magazine and spoke to the woman in a lower voice. "I can do what you wish," he said, "but it will be expensive."

"How expensive?" said the tall woman.

The stranger took out a pack of foul-smelling French cigarettes. Because the day was cloudy, he decided against the magnifying glass and lit one with a match. He inhaled deeply.

"I shall require that a fifty-thousand-dollar down payment be placed into a secret piggy bank in a locker in the Toledo bus station," he said, exhaling putrid French smoke. "When the job is done, I shall call and inform you. You will deposit another fifty thousand into the secret piggy bank. When I hear that the first fifty thousand has been deposited, I shall swing into action. I will not tell you what I'm going to do nor how I'm going to do it. I shall simply disappear off the face of the earth. You will hear nothing from me at all until I call to inform you that the job is finished. You will tell no one anything about this operation, and as soon as I leave, you will forget everything I have told you. You will completely erase it from your memory. If not, I will hear about it and I will be forced to kill you. Is that understood?"

"If I forget everything you told me," said the tall woman, "how can I remember what to do in order to pay you the rest of your money?"

"Okay, *don't* forget everything I told you," said the stranger. "Just forget *some* of the things I told you. *Most* of the things I told you. But not *all* of the things I told you."

"Which things should I forget and which things should I remember?" asked the tall woman.

"Forget everything but the part about how and where to pay me," said the stranger.

"That was pretty much all you told me," said the tall woman.

"Are you sure?" said the stranger.

"Pretty sure," said the tall woman.

"All right then," said the stranger. "In that case, remember *everything* I told you."

"Everything?" said the tall woman.

"Everything," said the stranger.

"Do you want me to remember what you look like?" the tall woman asked.

"Do you think this is what I look like?" said the stranger, with a mocking smile. He reached under his chin, grabbed an edge of the rubber mask, and ripped it right off his face. "*This* is what I look like," he said.

"That's amazing," said the tall woman. "How much your face looks like the mask, I mean."

"You think it looks like the mask?"

"Pretty much," said the tall woman. "Except for the mustache."

"You honestly believe this is my real face?" said the stranger. "You think the Master of a Thousand Disguises would reveal his true face to somebody he just *met*?"

"Okay, maybe not," said the tall woman.

"Well, all *right* then," said the stranger, with obvious satisfaction.

"All right, folks, that's it," said the old man. "Either buy the magazines or move on."

"We're moving on," said the stranger. He turned smartly on his heel and left.

# Wally, the World's Biggest Optimist

"Wally, I'm so pumped that you gave up being negative because I didn't die," said Cheyenne.

They were standing in the Spydelles' kitchen, doing the dinner dishes, Wally washing and Cheyenne drying. Outside it had started to rain. There was a gentle patter against the kitchen window.

"So far it's been easier than I thought," said Wally. "I realize now you probably weren't in too much danger of dying when you were running that high fever. I mean, you're young, you've got a great immune system—your body can handle almost any virus that attacks it if you just give it a chance."

"You're amazing," she said. "I can't believe the change that's come over you."

She reached over to hug him, and the dish she was drying slipped out of her hands. It fell on a pile of already dried dishes, and all of them crashed to the floor, smashing into a million pieces.

"Ooops," said Cheyenne.

"Hey, no problem," said Wally. "They're only dishes, and Shirley seems to have a ton of those. It could have happened to anyone. I'll clean it up for you." He stooped down and began to collect the broken pieces.

"Thanks," she said. "You know, you've never talked this way before."

"Well, that's the new me. I'm so sick of the old me. He was a downer. I mean,"—he chuckled—"the old me would be really worried now about what happened last night, right? About what made you go to the cave of the Ont Queen?"

"Actually," she said, "even *I'm* worried about that."

"You are?" he said. "Well, *that's* a relief! So can we drop this stupid positive stuff now?"

"You think being positive is stupid?" she asked, looking like she'd been slapped. She sneezed and blew her nose.

"Oh, uh, no," he said, "not at all. I just meant trying to be positive about the Ont Queen seems stupid. But you agree we need to find out as fast as possible what happened to you there and what the Ont Queen is up to?"

"Well, of course, Wally. I'm not an idiot, you know."

# CHAPTER 8

# Poisons "Я" Us

Cincinnati is the city that gave the world Play-Doh, Formica, floating soap, oral polio vaccine, and the Heimlich maneuver, but all it could come up with this day was a relentless, windy downpour that soaked shoes, ruined hairdos, and turned umbrellas inside out. The figure in the mirrored sunglasses and the black leather trench coat made its way along the narrow rain-swept street to the address on the card in his black-gloved paw. The flaked and faded silver lettering on the storefront window spelled out PATRIOTIC ALL-AMERICAN INSTRUMENT CO., FOUNDED 1945.

The store looked dark, but when the stranger tried the door, it creaked open. The stranger entered. The gloomy shop was crammed with musical instruments of every imaginable shape, from tiny silver fifes to sensuous brass saxophones to gigantic tubas with serpentine coils of dull yellow metal. The shop smelled like tarnished silverware that hadn't been polished in decades.

A gnome with a shaved and shiny head appeared out of the gloom. He wore a steel-rimmed monocle jammed in his right eye.

"Ze store iss clozed," the gnome hissed with a heavy European accent.

"And yet the door was open," said the stranger.

"A regrettable miztake," said the gnome, "for vich zomebody vill pay dearly." He locked the door. "Zince you haff succeeded in barging in here, vat do you vish?"

"I am looking for something in an amusingly lethal poison," said the stranger.

The gnome could see miniature reflections of his shiny head in the lenses of the stranger's sunglasses, but he couldn't see the stranger's eyes. Outside, the rain grew stronger, as if some-one had turned up the dial on a bathroom shower.

"You haff come to ze wrong place," said the gnome. "You must go to a poison store. You can find zem in ze Yellow Pages."

"I was told that *you* sell poisons," said the stranger.

"Somebody hass been pulling your leg," said the gnome. "Tveaking your nose. Putting you on, yes? Ve haff no poisons here, only muzical inztruments."

"What a pity," said the stranger. He took out a pack of stinky brown French cigarettes. He set a hundred-dollar bill on fire and used it to light his cigarette. "Now I shall have to spend all this money somewhere else." He opened a small black bag to reveal neatly rubber-banded bricks of newly minted hundred-dollar bills.

The rain flung itself fitfully against the shop windows, as if frantic to get inside the warm, dry shop. The gnome considered the tidy packages of hundred-dollar bills in the black bag.

"If ve *did* carry ze poisons," said the gnome, "vich ve certainly do not, vat kind vould you haff had in mind?"

"Something that produces a short period of intense suffering and then a painful and grotesque death," said the stranger.

The gnome took out a pack of stinky brown Turkish cigarettes, fitted one into a long silver cigarette holder, and lit it with a flaming thousand-dollar bill.

"Although ve zell only muzical inztruments," said the gnome, exhaling a cloud of putrid smoke in the stranger's direction, "zometimes, as a courtezy to our cuztomers, ve carry alzo a few poisons."

The stranger allowed the smoke to drift past him and then, without raising his voice or betraying emotion of any kind, said, "If you blow smoke in my face again, I shall squeeze your neck until your face turns black and your tongue falls out. I shall then go to your home, kill every member of your family and all of your houseplants. Is that understood?"

The gnome gulped and nodded. "It iss understood."

"Excellent," said the stranger. "Now then, what sort of poisons do you carry?"

"Ve haff ze venom of ze black mamba," said the gnome nervously, "a snake zat grows fourteen feet in length und iss so aggressive zat it rears up to strike und can bite a human on ze face. Ze black mamba venom iss a hundred percent fatal. Ve haff also ze venom of ze death adder, vich iss only fifty percent fatal, but ze name *death adder* iss so perky zat ve carry it anyway. Ve haff ze venom of ze spitting cobra, vich seldom bites but spits venom into its victim's eyes. Und ve haff ze venom of ze most poisonous snake in ze vorld, ze taipan snake from Australia. Vun bite iss enough to kill a hundred full-grown men."

The stranger sighed wearily. "Snake venom seems so . . . *common*," he said. "What about spiders?"

"Oh, ve haff *luffly* spiders," said the gnome. "Ve haff ze black vidow spider—whose favorite trick iss to hide under ze seat of an outhouse und bite its victim on ze tushy. Ve haff ze brown recluse spider, vich iss deadlier zan most poisonous snakes. Ve haff ze funnel-veb spider, vich iss ze deadliest spider in ze vorld. Ve haff ze venom of ze wasp jellyfish, vich kills ten times as many people every year as ze great vhite shark."

"I'm afraid all venom sounds unbearably . . . *last year,*" said the stranger. "I'm a professional. I have a reputation to think of. I'm looking for something a little more *fun.* Don't you have something that hasn't been done to death?"

"Yess," said the gnome. "Zis veek only ve haff a special on insulin—ven given in extreme overdose, it causes insulin shock. Symptoms are immediate: thirst, nausea, redness in ze face, chills, extreme nervousness, shallow breathing, rapid und irregular heartbeat, sveating, fatigue, dizziness, coma, und finally, death. Vould you be interested in zomezing like zat?"

"Insulin shock," the stranger repeated. "I do like the sound of that. All right then, here are my terms." The little warmth that had been present

in the stranger's voice was now squeezed out of
it like juice from an overripe lime. "I shall pay
you twice as much for the insulin as it is worth,
and you will forget who bought it from you. You
will forget that I was here at all. You will never

speak of this incident to anyone. If you do, I shall hear about it, and I shall kill you and everyone you have ever known, including your grandma, your postal carrier, and your orthodontist. Is that understood?"

The gnome gulped and nodded. "It iss understood."

## CHAPTER 9

# Down the Rabbit Hole

The more he thought about the Ont Queen's cave, the more Wally wanted to know what was going on there. He knew how dangerous it would be to go back again, especially if he managed to get inside, but he had to find out what the onts were up to.

The onts clearly had some weird control over Cheyenne, and they were obviously still plotting to replace mankind with a race of giant ants. He owed it to his family and to the whole human race to try to stop them, even if doing so endangered his life. He knew Cheyenne would go with him if he asked her, but decided not to risk her safety. If there was trouble at the cave, losing *one* kid would be bad enough for Dad and the Spydelles.

Shortly after breakfast, Wally pocketed his Swiss Army knife and slipped out of the Spydelles' house. He told neither Cheyenne nor Shirley where he was going.

The trail they'd taken through the forest from the Ont Queen's cave the other night wasn't hard to follow. Wally recognized enough landmarks to keep him on course. The day was warm and very humid, and before long his brisk pace caused his skin to prickle with perspiration. Bluebottle flies buzzed and bumbled about his face. Mosquitoes, drawn by the delicious fragrance of human sweat, flew into his ears, their annoying high-pitched whine causing him to keep slapping his face until it was red.

In less than half an hour, he saw the entrance. In the bright sunlight and without the fog, it looked much different: a low hill covered by grass, with an arched opening that was deep in shadow. If he squinted, it looked like an openmouthed shark.

Taking care to remain unseen by anyone who might be watching, Wally circled the mouth of the cave from a distance of at least fifty feet. Yes, he could now make out at least two guards chatting in the dark shade of the cave's mouth, so going in this way wasn't possible.

But Wally knew there could be many entrances to a cave. He knew caves were formed by water, so he searched for a nearby stream that might feed into it. He found one soon and followed it to a spot on the side opposite the main entrance, to a hole in the ground that looked as though it led into the cave. The hole was just big enough for a ten-year-old to climb through, so Wally did.

He dropped down several feet, landing with a tremendous splash in an underground pool. The water was icy and made him shiver. He swam to the edge of the pool and climbed out. His clothes were drenched, but that felt refreshing on such a hot, humid day. He looked around.

Wally had fallen into a natural underground grotto with a high ceiling. The only source of light came from the hole in the ceiling through which he'd dropped. A steady waterfall poured from hole to pool, creating a pleasant gurgling sound that echoed in the grotto. He could see no tunnels leading out. The grotto didn't seem to be connected to the cave of the Ont Queen as he had hoped.

*It probably isn't the greatest time to think of this,* he said to himself, *but what if the only way out of here is that hole in the ceiling I just dropped through? There's no way I could ever climb back up there. Who knows I'm here? Not Cheyenne or Shirley. Not Dad or Edgar.* Nobody *knows I'm here. Nobody will hear me if I yell for help, not even the onts. I'll starve to death. They'll find me eventually, but by then I'll be a rotting skeleton with a snake wriggling through one of my eyeholes. Okay, Wally, cut it out. That's negative thinking, and I promised if Cheyenne lived, I wouldn't do that anymore. So, all right, I'm deciding that there is* another *way out of here, and I'm just going to look for it until I find it.*

The walls and ceiling of the grotto were rough rock. Several birds *flup-flup*ped past Wally's head, and then he realized that they weren't birds but bats. A ripple of creepiness started at his scalp and scooted down his back. *Boys who have vampire fathers are not allowed to be creeped out by bats,* he told himself.

At floor level on the far end of the grotto was another hole. He walked over to it and crouched down. Dozens of flat oval things skittered away from him on the rocky floor. *Giant cockroaches? Yuck!*

He knelt down and stuck his head into the hole. It seemed to be a passageway of some sort. If he got down on his stomach, he could just fit into it. Should he? In the grotto there was space; there was even a little light. In the passageway there was neither. In the grotto there was nothing for him but starvation. In the passageway there was neither space nor light, but through it he might possibly find a way out.

Wally crawled into the passageway. It was so tight, he could barely breathe. *What if I get stuck?* he wondered. *Wouldn't dying that way be worse than dying out in the grotto? C'mon, Wally, cut it out.*

Pulling himself forward on his elbows, he began crawling through the passageway. After a few yards, it widened a little. *Okay, things are looking up,* he thought. Then something began to creep slowly across his hand.

Something large. Something slithery.

He shuddered. Was it a lizard? A snake? A rattlesnake? What if it bit him? From his compulsive reading of encyclopedias while at the Jolly Days Orphanage, he remembered that ninety-eight percent of all snakebites in the United States are from rattlesnakes. The venom caused nausea, vomiting, excessive thirst, difficulty breathing, paralysis, and death. The thing for him to remember was, whether it was a rattlesnake or not, it was more afraid of *him*. Oh yeah, right!

The large, slithery creature, whatever it was, continued its unhurried journey across his hand and then his arm, and then it disappeared. *All right, things are definitely improving,* he thought. At that moment the ground gave way beneath him.

He dropped several feet to an earthen floor and yelped with pain. His knees and the palms of his hands felt as though they were on fire, but he was relieved to find no jagged pieces of bone were poking through his flesh. He was lucky. He looked about.

Wally had fallen straight into a tunnel with smoothly rounded walls and ceiling. Had he made it into the Ont Queen's underground fortress?

# CHAPTER 10

# Whatever You Do, Stay Out of the Dairy

Wally got up slowly and began limping rapidly along the tunnel.

Oil lamps hung from the walls and provided scarcely enough light to see. The air smelled like wet earth, a not unpleasant smell. More tunnels branched off in several directions.

Wally chose one at random and began walking. The tunnel descended at a fairly steep angle. The farther the tunnel descended, the harder and smoother the walls and floor became. After about a hundred yards, the hard-packed earth gave way to white ceramic tile.

A round steel door in the tunnel wall was marked NURSERY. Wally opened the door a few inches and peered inside. He beheld a vast room filled with hundreds of long stainless steel shelves. On the shelves were row upon row of large open-topped boxes that looked like milk cartons, just like the ones he'd discovered in the Mandible House cellar. Thousands of cartons, attended by a crew of worker onts in blue scrub suits. Thousands of cartons, inhabited by thousands of eyeless, slimy, gray, sharp-toothed, puppy-sized larvae. A worker ont looked up and saw Wally.

"Hey!" said the worker ont. "Who let *you* in here?"

Wally slammed the door and beat it down the tunnel as fast as he could go.

The door opened and two worker onts stuck their heads out. "See?" said the one who'd yelled at him. "I told you! It's a human!"

They started running after him.

*You do not want to get captured by angry onts in their underground fortress,* Wally thought as he ran. It was a long tunnel, there didn't seem to be any offshoots branching away from it, and they were gaining on him.

"Halt!" shouted a worker ont. "I command you to halt!"

*Yeah, right,* Wally thought. *Halting is really going to happen here. Halting is something I would seriously consider doing.*

He kept running, breathing hard, breathing fast, legs pumping, heart thumping. He looked over his shoulder. The two worker onts were keeping up with him, but they were no longer gaining on him. *Good!* He might just make it, unless other onts suddenly appeared, running toward him from the opposite direction.

*Uh-oh.*

Other onts suddenly appeared, running toward him from the opposite direction.

Immediately to his right was a round steel door marked DAIRY. He opened it, leaped through it, slammed it, and locked it behind him.

Someone tried the doorknob.

"It's locked!" said a voice.

There was banging on the dairy door.

"Open up!" someone shouted.

"Do you have a key?" asked someone else. "Well then, go and *get* one!"

He had entered a huge, dimly lit room filled with . . . At first he didn't even know what they were; he knew only that the sight of them made him want to throw up. Dozens of bloated, disgusting-looking beetles the size of sheep! Beetles with waving antennae and six buggy legs and swollen teardrop-shaped bodies that were nearly transparent. Clear plastic tubes ran from the creatures' bodies into long stainless steel tanks.

Wally was momentarily mystified. And then he realized what they must be—giant aphids! From his study of the *A*s in the encyclopedia back at Jolly Days, he knew that ants milk aphids for nutritious fluid called honeydew, and keep them in their colonies the way humans keep cows.

"Okay, I got the key," said a voice outside.

"Good," said a second voice.

Wally heard the sound of a key being inserted into a lock.

He looked frantically around the dairy, seeking another way out. On the far side of the room was a back door, but dozens of giant aphids blocked his path. He sure didn't want to push through them to get to it, but there didn't seem to be any other choice. He took a deep breath and walked forward.

# CHAPTER 11

# What Shall We Do with the Humans Who Resist Slavery?

Squeezing between the bloated aphid bodies was like squeezing between huge water balloons, except that the balloons were aphids and they were alive and filled with disgusting honeydew aphid juice.

By the time the worker onts got the door open, Wally had reached the back door. He tore it open, slammed it behind him, and took off down another tunnel. Before he'd gone more than the length of a football field, he heard voices.

"...but the problem with the human race is not only that they are polluting the earth, the air, and the water, Your Highness," said one voice. "In the rural areas, their coal mining operations endanger our underground communities, and in the cities it's their tunnels and their subway systems."

Somebody was talking to the Ont Queen herself! He looked around to see where the voices were coming from. *There!* In the wall ahead of him on the right was a square metal frame with a screen over the opening. An air duct. *The voices must be coming from there!*

"Did you know that in New York the ont colony beneath Flushing, Queens, had to be relocated because of a subway station?" said another voice.

"Did we not tell you we had broken off communication with the ont colony in Queens?" said a stronger, deeper voice. "Have you been communicating with them in deliberate violation of our orders?"

"N-no, My Queen," said the voice. "I would never disobey your orders. I heard about this from one of the army onts."

"Very well," said the queen. "Yes, the humans'

misguided actions are a problem for onts everywhere. Once we enslave them, the problem will
be solved."

"How will we enslave them, Your Highness?"
asked another voice. "Will we keep them the
way we keep the aphids?"

"No, no," said the queen. "We shall keep
them the way that our cousins, the slavemakers,
keep the ants they conquer. The slavemaker ants
force their slaves to groom and feed their queen,
to tend to their babies, to gather food, and to
defend the colony from attack. If the colony
moves, the slaves carry their masters to the new
home on their backs."

"What will we do with the humans who
resist slavery, My Queen?" asked yet another
voice.

The queen laughed raucously.

"Why, we shall do what humans do to ants,
of course," she said. "Exterminate them!"

Wally shuddered.

"And do we have a plan for how to do that,
Your Highness?"

"Oh, most emphatically," said the queen.

Wally wanted to find out how the onts were planning to exterminate the humans, but then he heard the sounds of somebody coming.

He looked up at the air duct. The cover was held in place by four screws. He took out his Swiss Army knife, flipped out the screwdriver blade, and began unscrewing screws as fast as he could, dropping them on the floor. He lifted off the cover of the air duct and climbed into the duct, just as three worker onts came into view.

"Look!" one shouted. "Somebody's escaping into the wall! Is that a human?"

"It couldn't be!"

Wally began crawling frantically in the confined space of the air duct as the voices approached the opening. His knees and elbows were making an awful racket in the tin duct, and he worried that the queen and those who were with her would hear it. He kept on going, having no idea of where the duct was taking him, but also having no choice but to continue crawling.

He heard the worker onts enter the air duct and start noisily after him.

The duct Wally was crawling through was hot, and he began sweating heavily. It turned abruptly to the right, and then shot straight upward. Fortunately, there was a ladder with iron rungs in the vertical section, and he began to climb it.

*How close they sound now!* The worker onts must have been crawling faster than Wally was. They were gaining ground much too quickly. He climbed and climbed, getting shorter and shorter of breath, streaming sweat into his eyes, his mouth. The sounds were softer—the worker onts must have reached the base of the ladder. Now they were beginning to climb.

He kept propelling himself upward till his head collided with something solid. A grate. A grate with sunlight streaming through its bars! He tried to lift the grate so he could climb through it, but it wouldn't budge. It must have been screwed in place, but he couldn't see the screws. That meant they must be on the other side!

*Okay, Wally, this isn't looking too terrific. This could be the end of everything...*

He took out his Swiss Army knife again, snapped out the screwdriver, and reached it up through the grate. It was hard to squeeze his hand through the bars, hard to locate the first screw, harder yet to fit the tip of the screwdriver into the first slot and drive it, but he finally did. And then the second one.

Closer—the worker onts were climbing up the ladder, coming closer!

Wally got the tip of the blade into the second screw and turned it till the screw came out.

And then the third. The screwdriver kept slipping out of the third slot, and now they were almost upon him. He finally got the third screw turning, but there wasn't going to be time for the fourth.

He tried it anyway. An ont worker reached up with her claws and grabbed his ankle. Wally kicked out and broke her grip.

He tried to maneuver the screwdriver into the fourth screw, but ont claws were once more

85

grasping at his ankles. The blade of the screwdriver finally found its slot, but when he tried to turn it, he found the screw frozen. It must have rusted solidly in place!

Now two claws grabbed his ankles and held them tight. He kicked free again, and with all his might shoved upward against the grate, creating an opening almost big enough to crawl through. He pushed even harder against the grate, bending the rusty screw backward till it snapped and the grate came off in his hands.

Wally grabbed the edges of the square hole above his head and *puuuuullllled* himself upward, kicking wildly at the claws that tried to hold him. When his head and shoulders cleared the opening, he thrust himself forward onto warm grass.

He yanked his legs out of the hole, raised himself into a runner's racing crouch, and took off through the forest in the direction of home.

# CHAPTER 12

# Beware of Strangers
# Bearing Inoculations

"Since you've chosen me as your new adoptive mother," said Shirley, settling herself on Cheyenne's bed, "I thought we might speak a little of the rich spider heritage we will now be sharing. How much do you already know about us spiders?"

"Well," said Cheyenne, "Wally told me black widow spiders' venom is fifteen times more poisonous than rattlesnakes'."

"Yes," said Shirley, "and did you know that if a black widow spider were human sized, like me, its venom could wipe out an entire continent?"

"How wonderful!" said Cheyenne, clapping her hands.

"Why would it be wonderful to wipe out an entire continent?" asked Shirley, frowning.

Cheyenne looked embarrassed. "Oh, um, well, it wouldn't be, of course. Unless, you know, it was a really *bad* continent and it was planning to use weapons of mass destruction on us or something."

Shirley continued to frown.

"And probably not even then," said Cheyenne. "It wouldn't be wonderful at all. It would be horrible. Oh, I've got a question. Are Wally and me now related to all spiders, just like total strangers become your cousins when your dad marries somebody new?"

"That might have been the case if I'd been *born* a spider," said Shirley. "But I wasn't. As I think you already know, I was born human and only became a spider after I died from a spider bite and Edgar brought me back to life again with his Elixir of Life."

Cheyenne frowned and began twisting a strand of her hair.

"So if I wanted to become part spider," said

Cheyenne, "I'd have to convert to arachnidism or something?"

"Uh, yes." Shirley nodded. "Anyway, spiders have been on this planet for three hundred and fifty thousand years. We know of at least thirty-seven thousand species of spiders worldwide, and seven hundred species now live in Florida. We've become friendly with a lovely family in Miami that we see every winter. The mother, Estelle, a black widow, makes us a tasty dish that she taught me to prepare, Stuffed Jellied Sirloin Steak."

"That sounds yummy," said Cheyenne, letting her hair untwist. "Could you teach me to prepare it?"

"I suppose so," said Shirley. "What I do is, I inject the steak with my saliva, which turns the inside of it to jelly. Then I . . . On second thought, I'd better start you out on something easier. Which reminds me, dear—it's nearly lunchtime. What would you like for lunch?"

"I don't know," said Cheyenne, playing with her hair again. She sneezed and blew her nose. "What have you got?"

"What about chunky soup?" said Shirley. "I think some lovely soup would be the perfect thing for a girl who's recovering from a serious case of the flu."

"Gosh, I don't know if I'm in the mood for soup," said Cheyenne.

"No?" said Shirley. "Just imagine. Lovely, nutritious soup. Lovely warm liquid filling you right up. Lovely warm liquid spreading from the tips of your toes to the top of your head."

"Lovely warm liquid spreading from the tips of my toes to the top of my head," murmured Cheyenne. "Yesss . . ."

"Good girl," said Shirley. She left the bedroom to prepare the soup.

Cheyenne slumped to the floor in a deep trance.

Just as Shirley entered the kitchen to make lunch, Wally ran in breathlessly from outside. He was covered with sweat and dirt, and his clothes were wet and torn.

"Wally," said Shirley, "where have you been?

And why do you look like you've been wrestling alligators?"

"It's a long story, Shirley," he said. "Let me clean up now, and then I'll tell you all about it. Do you have anything to eat? I'm starving."

"I've just begun making lunch for Cheyenne. What would you like to eat?"

"Anything that's not jellied," he said. "Oh, sorry, Shirley. Was that too negative?"

"Not at all," said Shirley. "What about some nice soup?"

"Whatever," said Wally. "No, I mean soup would be great. But do you have anything I could eat right now? Because I really am starving."

She handed him a Choco-Doodle-Doo bar. "I was saving this for dessert," she said, "but you can have one bite now so you don't starve. Don't eat any more or it'll spoil your appetite."

"Thanks, Shirley," said Wally.

He took the chocolate bar and went into the bathroom to clean up. He took one bite and began to chew. It was ridiculously delicious. He started to take another bite, then remembered his promise. He put the uneaten bar down on the sink, turned on the water, and began washing.

In the kitchen Shirley took down a large iron pot and then looked in the cabinet for a couple of cans of chunky chicken noodle soup. But the last can had been consumed the day before.

"Wally!" Shirley called. "We're fresh out of soup. I'm going to the store to buy more, okay?"

"Okay, Shirley," Wally answered from the bathroom.

Shirley left the house for the short walk to Dripping Fang Groceries and Sundries.

A few minutes after she had left, the front doorbell rang. Wally continued washing up. The doorbell rang again, insistently.

"Hold on a second, will you?" Wally yelled.

He put on a clean shirt and jeans, dropped the chocolate bar into the pocket of his fresh shirt, ran a comb through his hair, and went to see who was at the door.

It was a stranger wearing a surgical mask,

green hospital scrubs, thin rubber gloves, and a stethoscope draped around his neck. Wally thought the stranger seemed unusually furry.

"Good afternoon," said the stranger. "I'm Dr. Black from the Centers for Disease Control." He flashed the official-looking plastic ID card that hung from a cord around his neck. "What is your name, please?"

"Wally. Wally Shluffmuffin."

"Excellent," said the stranger. "Well, Wally, I've come to inoculate all children in this area against the serious flu epidemic that's sweeping the Greater Cincinnati Area. It's a free injection." He took out a syringe with a very long needle. "Please drop your pants."

"You're kidding me," said Wally.

"All right then, roll up your sleeve," said the stranger.

"Look," said Wally, "my sister just got over a bad case of the flu, so I've already been exposed to it. I'm either going to get it or I'm not."

"If your sister survived," said the stranger,

"she didn't have the strain that we're inoculating against, which is ninety percent fatal."

Wally thought this over for a minute, then sighed. "The *old* me would have been suspicious," he said. "But this is the *new* me."

Wally rolled up his sleeve, and the stranger gave him a quick jab from his syringe. It felt like the sting of a wasp.

"There," said the stranger, "that wasn't so bad, was it?"

"I guess not," said Wally, trying to disguise his pain. "Sorry if I gave you a hard time. I'm trying not to be so negative anymore."

"No problem," said the stranger. "Are you feeling any reaction yet?"

"Oh, does it work that fast?"

"Sometimes."

"No, I . . . Wait a minute. Yeah," said Wally. "I *am* starting to feel a little weird."

"Can you describe what you're feeling?" the stranger asked eagerly.

"I'm just . . . feeling kind of funny," said Wally.

"Can you be any more precise than that?"

"I feel like I'm going to puke and I'm... thirsty and... nervous and... I've got the chills."

"Very interesting," said the stranger, studying Wally's face. "Yes, you're getting very red in the face. And you're sweating profusely, and your breathing is becoming quite shallow."

"What's happening to me?" Wally asked.

"Nothing that isn't supposed to happen," said the stranger.

Wally felt as though the ground under his feet had tilted upward. His legs suddenly turned to pudding, and he fell to the floor, unconscious.

The stranger took out his cell phone and dialed a prearranged number.

"The package has been delivered," said the stranger, with no emotion in his voice. "Please deposit final payment in the agreed-upon location."

# CHAPTER 13

# Tragedy Strikes Out
# with Bases Loaded

Hanging upside down from the rafters in the Spydelles' garage, Vampire Dad stretched, spread his leathery wings, and floated to the floor.

He had spent a sleepless night, endlessly replaying in his head the tape of himself telling Edgar that he was giving him official permission to adopt his children—and the one of himself telling the kids they'd be better off with the Spydelles as parents. When he'd said that, Cheyenne and Wally had looked as though they were in actual physical pain. How could he have done such a thing to them? What kind of a father was he?

He'd promised God that's what he'd do if Cheyenne lived. But what made him think God had accepted the deal? Did God say, "Okay, Sheldon, you've got yourself a contract?" He did not. For all he knew, God hadn't even been listening to him, hadn't known there was an agreement at all. What if the reason Cheyenne survived was that she simply had a good immune system? Would it be fair for him to give up all hope of being a father again because of *that*?

Maybe it wasn't too late to take back what he'd said. Maybe it wasn't too late to tell his kids he loved them too much to give them to anyone else, even if he'd promised God. Sure, why not!

He left the garage and strode toward the house. Halfway there he noticed that the door of the house was ajar and somebody was lying just inside the doorway. Who was it? Was it . . . Wally? Oh no! It couldn't be!

Dad sprinted across the lawn and stopped short in the doorway. It *was* Wally! He scooped him up in his arms, but the boy was cold and lifeless, limp as linguine. What had happened? Had he died of a broken heart on hearing that his father no longer loved him? Was he dead? Or maybe he'd simply fallen asleep on the floor in the hallway. Yeah, right.

"Wally!" Dad shouted. "Wally, wake up!"

Wally neither moved nor answered. Dad burst into tears. Was God punishing him for thinking of breaking their deal? Could he revive him with CPR? He didn't *know* CPR. He knew it had something to do with blowing into an unconscious person's mouth, but he didn't know what to do after that—and he didn't want to do it wrong. He'd always meant to learn CPR someday, but he'd never really had the time. Now it was too late! He put the boy gently down on the floor and ran off to find help.

"Edgar!" he shouted. "Wally needs CPR! Do you know CPR?"

Edgar didn't answer. Where was Edgar? Edgar was at work in Cincinnati, of course, in the Cincinnati Museum of Natural History!

"Shirley!" he shouted. "Wally needs CPR! Do you know CPR?"

Shirley didn't answer. Why didn't she answer? Where was Shirley? Did giant spiders know CPR?

Call an ambulance! Call 911! Where was the phone? There it was! He grabbed the phone and punched in 911.

"This is Sheldon Shluffmuffin!" he screamed into the receiver. "I'm at the Spydelle house in Dripping Fang Forest just outside Cincinnati, and I need an ambulance here immediately!"

"This is Information. What city and state, please?" It was a recording.

*Information?* Had he punched 411 instead of 911?

He slammed the receiver down, picked it up, and dialed again.

"We're sorry, your call did not go through," said another recorded voice. "Please hang up and dial again."

Dad swore violently, slammed the receiver into its cradle, then dialed again, this time with deliberate, almost sarcastic slowness.

"You have reached a nonworking number in the Cincinnati area," said yet another recorded voice. "If you feel you have received this message in error, please hang up, check the number, and dial again."

Dad threw the phone against the wall and raced around the house in a blind panic, desperately looking for help.

He ran into the kids' bedroom, and that's when he saw Cheyenne's lifeless body on the floor.

"Cheyenne! Oh no! Oh my god, no! Not you, too!" he shouted. "Wake up, Cheyenne! Wake up!"

He gathered up her lifeless body in his arms. *See if she has a pulse. You can find a pulse in her carotid artery. The carotid artery is in the neck.* He tried to find her carotid artery, but forgot where on the neck it was located and felt nothing.

"My poor children are both dead, probably of broken hearts!" he sobbed. "This is all my fault! Without Wally and Cheyenne, I no longer want to live! I wish to end this mockery of a life, but I'm already dead—how can a vampire commit suicide?"

Dad tenderly placed Cheyenne's body back down on the floor. Then he ran into the kitchen. He fumbled through the tool drawers, tossing screwdrivers, hammers, pliers, and crescent wrenches in all directions, looking for what he needed. He finally located a mallet and a wooden stake.

He lay down on the kitchen floor. He did a quick survey of his chest, and with one hand placed the sharp end of the stake where he thought his heart ought to be. With his other hand, he seized the mallet and, with three powerful blows, drove the stake directly into his heart.

# CHAPTER 14

# Why It Pays to Memorize Encyclopedias

It was the oddest sensation. Lying on the hallway floor, looking up at the ceiling, Wally's field of vision looked exactly like a TV screen that had shrunk till it was the size of one you could wear on your wrist. Funny, he'd always wanted a wrist TV.

He had watched the melodrama of his distraught Dad take place above him a moment ago, but he had been powerless to answer, and besides, the image was so tiny and so far away, it hardly seemed important. At some level Wally knew that consciousness was slipping away from him, and that when the wrist-sized TV grew tiny enough, it would make a soft popping sound and go out—and that would be the end of him.

Yet another benefit of his being an avid encyclopedia reader was that Wally pretty much knew by heart the symptoms of many fatal conditions. Before the picture on his imaginary wrist TV went out, he reviewed his symptoms. Let's see, there was thirst, nausea, reddening of the face, chills, nervousness, shallow breathing, rapid and irregular heartbeat, sweating, fatigue, dizziness . . . These seemed like the symptoms of some kind of poisoning. Had the guy from the CDC given him poison? Why would he have done that? More important, what kind of poison could it have been?

Maybe it was the castor bean. "Even two castor beans, well chewed, can be fatal," he remembered reading. But the symptoms? "Burning in the mouth, nausea, vomiting, cramps, sleepiness, convulsions, coma, and death." He had no burning in his mouth. It wasn't castor beans.

Was it lily of the valley? All parts of the pretty

green plant with the little white bell-shaped flowers are poisonous. Symptoms? "Hot flushes, irritability, headache, red skin patches, cold clammy skin, nausea, excess saliva, hallucinations . . ." He didn't have either excess saliva or hallucinations. It wasn't lily of the valley.

Hemlock poisoning, he remembered, causes lots of muscle pain, which he didn't have. Venom of the brown recluse spider causes blisters and blue-tinged skin, which he also didn't have. Gila monster venom causes blue-tinged skin, vertigo, and ringing in the ears, none of which he had. He sped through several dozen more lists of symptoms, then realized that his were identical to those of . . . insulin shock.

Wally mentally summoned up a quote from the encyclopedia: "Insulin shock may be followed by coma and, eventually, death." The antidote to insulin shock swam into view on his wrist TV as well: "The sugar in either hard candy or a chocolate bar will counteract the insulin and reduce the symptoms."

He remembered the Choco-Doodle-Doo bar

in his shirt pocket, which seemed forty miles away, and he wondered how he would ever be able to reach it before the screen shrank more and popped and the light went out forever. Could he even move his hand? He tried. He could not.

Could he move as many as two of his fingers? One, definitely. Two, possibly.

He tried. He succeeded in walking his fingers slowly, slowly across his chest, a half inch at a time, finally arriving at the pocket, but he'd used up all his energy in the trip and had none left to insert them into the pocket. The wrist TV shriveled, flickered, and threatened to pop.

He tried his pocket and was able to finally insert two trembling fingers, grasp the edge of the candy wrapper, and slowly, slowly pull it out.

Now what? How to get the chocolate bar from where it lay on his chest into his mouth? He certainly didn't have the strength to tear off the wrapper and jam it between his jaws, but maybe, just maybe, he had the strength to drag the bar up six inches to his mouth. Yeah, that's it. Just a little farther. One more inch and the edge of the wrapper was brushing his lips.

With a mammoth effort of will, Wally opened his lips, clamped them around the bar, and maneuvered it into his mouth. The TV screen was now no more than a bright dot. He chewed down on the Choco-Doodle-Doo bar, wrapper and all, and felt his teeth puncture the paper, felt that first sweet tiny taste of chocolate, felt the tiniest spark of energy, just enough to make it possible for him to open his jaws and close them back down again.

Another spark of strength, this time stronger. His jaws worked faster and faster, and soon he'd chewed and swallowed the entire bar, wrapper and all.

A surge of strength coursed through his body. Wally sat up.

# CHAPTER 15

# The Stake Is Not Our Best Today—May I Interest You in Something Else?

Her father's words, *"Wake up, Cheyenne!"* had stirred something deep in Cheyenne's unconscious mind. She began the long, laborious climb upward through hundreds of layers of sleepiness.

She recalled having had a terrible dream about her dad. Had he been upset with her? Was he in some kind of trouble?

Cheyenne swam to the surface of consciousness, broke through, and took a deep breath. Ahhhh!

———

Wally heard Cheyenne's scream and crawled painfully into the kitchen.

Cheyenne was semistanding, semileaning against the kitchen doorway, staring at the floor and continuing to scream. On the floor was Dad, a wooden stake sticking out of his chest, a wooden mallet in one hand, and a glassy-eyed stare on his face.

Both twins looked as though someone had smacked them in the stomach with a shovel.

"Poor Dad!" cried Wally. "It isn't fair! He had so much to live for. I mean, okay, technically he may have been dead for the past three years, but still, he had so much to . . . to be a member of the living dead for!"

"Why did he do this? Why?" sobbed Cheyenne. Tears spilled down her cheeks and made damp spots on her T-shirt.

"Maybe he saw me unconscious on the hall floor and thought I was dead," said Wally.

"Why were you unconscious on the floor?"

"A guy from the Centers for Disease Control

came by and gave me, um...some kind of a messed-up shot."

"Why'd he do that?"

"I don't know."

"Well, maybe Dad saw *me* unconscious on the bedroom floor and thought *I* was dead," said Cheyenne.

"Why were *you* unconscious on the floor?" asked Wally.

"I don't know," said Cheyenne. "I think I fainted or something."

"Well, probably he saw both of us," said Wally.

"Yeah, probably," said Cheyenne.

She couldn't stand looking at her father in this condition, but she couldn't tear her eyes away, either.

"The worst part," she said, "is that, even though he no longer wanted custody of us, Dad died believing we loved Edgar and Shirley more."

The screen door squeaked, and Shirley came into the house, carrying a brown bag filled with cans of chunky soup. When she caught sight of Dad on the floor, she screamed and dropped the bag. Cans of chunky soup rolled pell-mell everywhere.

"What happened?" Shirley cried.

"Dad committed suicide," sobbed Wally. "It's our fault. He saw us both unconscious on the floor, and he thought that we were dead."

"Why were you both unconscious on the floor?"

"It's too long a story to get into now," said Cheyenne.

Shirley knelt down and put two of her arms around each child and held them tightly as they cried and blew their noses.

"It's not your fault," said Shirley softly. "You're not to blame for this."

"Quite right," said a British voice behind them. "*I'm* the one who's to blame for your father's suicide. I killed him as surely as if I had wielded that mallet myself."

"Why, Edgar, what are *you* doing home so early?" asked Shirley.

"I promised God that if Cheyenne lived, I'd tell Sheldon the truth about the twins and why they said they wanted us to adopt them. But just as I began to speak, Sheldon interrupted me with his own declaration. Apparently, we all made separate deals with God for Cheyenne's deliverance. I was too weak to finish telling him what I'd begun to say, and I detest myself for it. All day at work I couldn't stop thinking about it. My conscience was troubling me so deeply, I came home early to tell him the truth. Sadly, I was not in time."

Shirley, Edgar, and the twins held one another for several moments, each sniffling and snuffling and blaming himself or herself for not living up to his or her promises.

"This may be indelicate," said Edgar at last, "but we ought to do something with the body. We jolly well can't take him to a funeral home, can we? There'd be all sorts of awkward questions about his having that wooden stake through his heart, being a vampire, and whatnot."

"What should we do?" asked Cheyenne.

"The best thing," said Shirley, "would be to give him a simple but dignified burial right here in the woods that he loved."

"Actually, I don't think Dad liked these woods at all," said Wally.

"That's not the point," said Shirley. "The point is we need to get him into the ground where he can finally find some peace. Let's get as many shovels as we can find and go around the back of the house to the garden."

## CHAPTER 16

# A Failure at Everything, Including Dying

The first clue Sheldon Shluffmuffin had that he might not be dead after all was an itch. The itch was in the area of his heart where the wooden stake had gone in. "I itch, therefore I am"—which French philosopher had said that? Descartes?

So his suicide had been a failure. "Not only was I a failure as a father, a zombie, and a vampire," Vampire Dad mused bitterly, "I can't even manage a simple suicide."

He pulled the stake out of his chest. Hmmm. Close inspection revealed that the wooden stake wasn't even wood; it was plastic with a printed wood-grain surface. Well, that explained a lot.

He rifled the drawers for pieces of real wood he could use as a stake, but the effort was futile. A long wooden ladle wasn't sharp enough to puncture his chest. Toothpicks and shish kebab sticks weren't strong enough to be pounded with a mallet.

Frustrated and angry, Dad recalled another way that vampires could be killed—silver bullets. He needed silver bullets and he needed a gun. He went to the Cincinnati Yellow Pages, looked up *Guns, Retail,* and found a listing for Ralphie's Guns 'n' Things. It wasn't too far away on the interstate, not too far away to hitchhike there.

He walked out the door and saw that the Spydelles' van was back. He jumped in and drove off.

An odd procession made its way along a trail in the dark forest: a long line of tall ladies wearing wide-brimmed black hats, black sunglasses, long black capes, and full-length black gloves, each with a burlap sack slung over her shoulder.

A pack of man-eating wolves, annoyed at being awakened from afternoon naps, poked their heads out of their dens to watch the procession as it passed. "How inconsiderate," said one, then went back to sleep.

A giant ten-foot-long slug stirred from its snooze under the bushes, opened an eye, and glared balefully at the procession, then returned to dreams of nibbling on orphans' feet. "Rude," said the slug. "Just plain rude is all it is."

When the procession reached the mouth of the Ont Queen's cave, army onts hustled the ladies inside and sped them and their precious cargo down the long, dank tunnels to a round steel door marked PRESS ROOM. Inside the press room, the burlap sacks were opened, and thousands of snot-filled tissues were shoveled into the loading bays of giant stainless steel presses.

"A good harvest today," remarked a worker ont.

"The best harvest so far," said a black-hatted ont, fishing a last crumpled Kleenex out of her sack. "Downtown Cincinnati was ankle deep in phlegm."

The loading bay doors clanged shut. The switches were thrown. The giant presses began squeezing out snot to feed the ravenous larvae.

"The babies will be so pleased," said the worker.

# CHAPTER 17

# The Exhaustive Screening Process We Must Endure Before Purchasing a Gun

"Okay, pal," said Ralphie, the troll who owned Ralphie's Guns 'n' Things, "Uncle Sammy says before I sellya a gun, I gotta askya a couple questions: You ever been in the joint?"

Dad looked around the shop, noting the impressive assortment of rifles, shotguns, handguns, and automatic weapons displayed on the walls—enough guns to take over a small South American country.

"You're asking me if I've ever been in a *joint*—in a disreputable place?" Dad asked.

Ralphie couldn't help noticing the sharpness of this customer's teeth and the hole in his chest. The fabric of his shirt ran right into the hole, which wasn't bleeding.

"No, no, no. I'm askin' did you ever do hard time?" said the troll.

"Oh, heavens, I've had *many* hard times," said Dad. "I wish I could tell you about some of them, but I'm in kind of a hurry now."

"What I'm askin' ya, pal," said the troll, "is did you ever go to prison for committin' a felony?"

"Prison?" said Dad. "Oh no, certainly not."

"Good," said the troll. "Congratulations, chief. Ya just bought yerself a gun."

He took a heavy bluish-black Smith & Wesson revolver out of the glass display case, breathed on it, and wiped off an imaginary fingerprint with the tail of his checkered flannel shirt. "Can I sellya some ammo?"

"Why yes," said Dad. "This might seem a foolish question, but would you happen to have any silver bullets?"

"You kidding me?" said the troll. "Chief, my motto is, If you shoot it, I sell it. How many silver bullets you need, Kemosabe?"

"Oh, one should be enough," said Dad.

He paid for the gun and the silver bullet, and went back to the Spydelles' van.

Edgar, Shirley, Cheyenne, and Wally trooped back into the kitchen, carrying among them a spade and two rusty shovels caked with dirt. It took them a few seconds to register that the body was no longer present.

"He's gone!" said Wally. "Dad's gone!"

"How is that possible?" said Edgar.

"Do you think somebody stole him?" said Shirley.

"Who'd steal a dead body?" said Cheyenne.

"A ghoul?" suggested Wally helpfully.

"There aren't any *ghouls* around here, silly," said Cheyenne.

"Actually there are," said Edgar. "The Boscos. But I believe they're currently on holiday in Italy."

"Maybe Dad recovered," Wally said. "Just got up and walked away."

"Not bloody likely," said Edgar. "You saw that stake through his heart. You don't just get up and walk away after something like that."

Cheyenne looked at Wally and cocked her head appreciatively. "That was a very positive thought, though, Wally," she said. "I like that."

Edgar glanced outside. "My word," he said. "The van's gone, too!"

They all ran outside, still carrying the shovels and spade, and stared at the place where the van had been.

"Do you think somebody put poor Sheldon's body in the van and drove off with it?" Shirley asked.

"Why would they do that?" asked Cheyenne.

"I don't know," said Shirley, "but we'd better call the police immediately."

"I agree," said Edgar, heading back indoors for the phone.

"Hold on a second," said Wally. "In case it *was*

Dad, who somehow recovered from his suicide, we wouldn't want the cops to arrest him, would we?"

Everybody stared at Wally.

"You honestly think your father could have recovered from a stake through the heart?" asked Edgar.

"Well, the *old* me wouldn't have thought so," said Wally.

"I have an idea," said Edgar. "Both our vehicles, the van and the new Land Rover, are equipped with Global Positioning System tracking devices, which I can monitor from my lab. Let's get on the monitor and see if we can locate the van. If it's not far from here, we could drive over there ourselves."

"Wouldn't it be dangerous to confront the thief who stole the van?" asked Shirley.

"I'm not afraid," said Wally.

"Neither am I," said Cheyenne.

They followed Edgar into his lab. On a long table was a row of glass beakers filled with liquids of many colors—turquoise, pink, purple, brown. Underneath each flask was a low blue flame that kept the liquids bubbling all day long. The brown one, Wally realized, was coffee.

They watched as Edgar turned on the GPS monitor. When the screen lit up, he adjusted some dials, and soon there appeared on the screen an outline map of the area around Dripping Fang Forest.

"Look," said Edgar. "See that little blinking red dot? That's the van!"

"Where is it?" asked Cheyenne.

"Not far from here," said Edgar. "Right off the interstate. It's stopped."

"Let's go get it," said Wally.


Sitting in the van's driver's seat, Vampire Dad placed the silver bullet in the cylinder, then put the barrel of the gun against his forehead. The cold metal left a small O imprinted in his flesh. He scrunched his eyes closed, and pulled the trigger.

The explosion was louder than an angry

door slam, and the recoil almost tore the gun out of his hand. But when the reverberations subsided, Dad found he was still conscious.

He placed the hot and smoking gun beside him on the seat. He gingerly touched the place on his forehead where he'd fired the shot and found a smooth round hole he could stick his finger into.

He got out of the van and walked unsteadily back into Ralphie's Guns 'n' Things.

"May I say something?" Dad asked.

"What?" said Ralphie, who had heard the shot outside and assumed the worst.

"Not to be discourteous," said Dad, "but I don't believe that what you sold me was a genuine one hundred percent pure silver bullet."

"Yeah, sure it was," said the troll uneasily, trying not to stare at the fresh, nonbleeding hole in Dad's forehead. "Okay, okay, ya got me. It was silver *plate*. So sue me—that's all I got. Pure silver is too soft to make bullets out of. What do you need pure silver for?"

"It's another story I don't have time to tell," said Dad. "But listen, is there a bridge anywhere near here with a very long drop to the water?"

"A bridge with a very long drop to the water," said the troll, stroking his warty chin. "Yeah, sure. Turn right and go about seven miles up the road. Ya can't miss it."

# CHAPTER 18

# How Do I Know Why He Wants a Bridge with a Long Drop to the Water?

As the Land Rover sped up the interstate, Shirley, Wally, and Cheyenne hunched over the GPS. The little blinking red dot was stopped on a wavy line that represented the interstate.

"We should be closing in on it any second now," said Edgar, trying to watch both the road and the GPS simultaneously. "Uh-oh."

"What happened to the blinking red dot?" said Wally.

"We just lost the signal," said Edgar. "That's all right, though. We should be making visual contact with the van any second now."

Up ahead on the right side of the highway was a small gravel parking lot and a store. A sign on the store read RALPHIE'S GUNS 'N' THINGS.

"That's odd," said Edgar. "This is where I estimated we'd find the van, but there isn't a single vehicle in the parking lot."

"Maybe it took off," said Cheyenne. "Maybe they knew we were coming."

"How could they possibly know we were coming?" said Wally.

"Hey, this is a gun store," said Cheyenne. "Maybe the thief stopped here to buy a gun."

"You mean *after* he stole the van?" said Shirley.

"Let's go in and ask," said Wally.

Edgar pulled the Land Rover into the parking lot. Everyone got out and rushed into the store. Everyone but Shirley, who took a little longer to get all her legs going in the right order.

"Howdy, folks," said Ralphie, trying not to seem surprised when Shirley, the enormous spider, entered his shop. "What can I do for you?"

"Was there a van in your parking lot a few minutes ago?" Wally asked.

"Yeah, as a matter of fact there was," said the troll.

"Could you describe the driver?" asked Wally.

"Sure," said the troll. "Skinny fella with very sharp teeth, wings, and holes in his chest and forehead."

"Dad!" shouted Cheyenne and Wally together, startling the troll, who feared they might be identifying him as their father.

"What was he doing here?" asked Shirley.

"Bought a gun and a silver bullet," said the troll. "Went out to the van for a while, then came back and asked me did I know if there was any bridges around here with a long drop to the water."

"What did you tell him?" asked Cheyenne.

"I says yeah, turn right and go about seven miles up the road—ya can't miss it."

"The man is suicidal," said Wally angrily. "Why didn't you try to stop him?"

"Why would I stop him?" asked the troll. "How do *I* know what he wants with a bridge

130

with a long drop to the water? Maybe he's a bungee jumper."

"C'mon," said Wally, racing for the door. "If we drive fast, we can get to the bridge before he jumps. The fall won't kill him, but it could break every bone in his body!"

They ran to the Land Rover and climbed in. Edgar stepped so hard on the accelerator, the car sprayed gravel as it left the lot.

# CHAPTER 19

# Don't Do Anything Rash

*I have nothing left to live for,* thought Dad as he got his first handhold on the structure of the bridge tower and began pulling himself upward. *Not that I'm technically alive, of course, but even if I were, I'd have nothing left to live for. My son and daughter are both dead. I myself am dead, and not in a good way, either. There's nothing for me here on Earth, so I might as well end it. I'll just climb to the very top of this bridge so that when I jump I'll have the best chance of dying—or whatever it is that vampires can do in that area—when I land.*

The suspension bridge spanned a seemingly bottomless canyon. A ten-story tower stood at each end of the roadway. Heavy steel cables curved between them, and the roadway hung from them by vertical cables. It was the tower on the near bank that Dad was climbing.

Dad continued climbing, hand over hand. The higher he climbed, the more the wind pulled and tugged at him and tried to yank him off the bridge. He looked downward. The river had taken several million years to carve its way through the rock walls, and the drop was now heart-stoppingly far. He wondered what it would feel like when he hit. Probably he wouldn't get a straight, clean drop all the way down. Probably he'd hit the canyon wall at about halfway there and ricochet.

In less than four minutes, they saw it up ahead of them: a suspension bridge spanning a deep gorge.

"There's somebody on the bridge!" shouted Wally. "See? Way up near the top! I think it's Dad!"

Indeed, a tiny figure clung to one tower of the bridge near the top.

133

"Hurry, Edgar, hurry!" cried Shirley.

"We've got to reach him before he has a chance to jump!" shouted Cheyenne.

A large truck lumbered in front of them, going no more than forty.

"There's a whole line of cars ahead of us," said Edgar. "I can't pass them."

"If you don't pass them," said Cheyenne, "Dad will jump before we get there."

The Land Rover pulled abruptly into the oncoming lane, passed the truck, passed a sedan and a station wagon and an SUV and another truck. A car in the oncoming lane hurtled toward them, growing larger by the second, horn blaring. They got back into the right lane with only seconds to spare, the passing car's angry horn sliding into a lower register as the car whooshed past them.

"Wow, Edgar, that was a little close!" said Wally. "In a good way, though," he added.

"You said to pass them," said Edgar, "so I passed them."

"And you did a really great job of it, too," said Wally.

The bridge was right ahead now, looming over their heads. Edgar pulled onto the shoulder and skidded to a stop, tires yerping. He, Wally, and Cheyenne were out of the car and running almost before it came to a complete stop.

"Dad!" Wally shouted, waving his arms wildly. "It's me, Wally! Don't jump!"

"Dad!" screamed Cheyenne. "It's me, Cheyenne! We're alive!"

Had he heard them? They couldn't tell. The tiny figure at the top of the bridge hadn't moved or responded in any way.

"Sheldon!" screamed Shirley. "It's me, Shirley! Please don't jump!"

"I say, Sheldon!" yelled Edgar. "It's Edgar! Don't do anything rash!"

"Dad, we love you!" Wally shouted.

"Dad, we need you!" Cheyenne shouted.

Far, far away, the tiny figure on the bridge waved back at them.

"He's waving!" screamed Cheyenne.

"He sees us!" Wally yelled.

The figure began slowly climbing downward.

"He's coming down!" shouted Cheyenne.

"He's not going to jump!" yelled Shirley.

"He's fallen!" shouted Edgar.

Indeed, the tiny figure had suddenly fallen off the bridge. In slow motion he ricocheted off the tower, then seemed to stick to it again, this time upside down.

"He must have slipped," said Shirley.

"He stopped his fall," said Wally.

"He's stuck up there," said Cheyenne.

"We have to save him!" yelled Wally.

# CHAPTER 20

# Saving Sheldon Shluffmuffin

Climbing upward, hand over hand, Wally, Cheyenne, Edgar, and Shirley were now more than halfway up the tower.

"Don't look down," Shirley advised.

It was windy up there, much windier than it had been on the ground. The wind whipped at their clothes, flapping them like flags. The entire bridge groaned and seemed to sway in the wind.

"Is this bridge swaying or what?" asked Cheyenne.

"Bridges sway," said Wally, who'd read about that in an encyclopedia, too. "Just like tall buildings. If they didn't, they'd crack apart."

"I'm not awfully keen on heights," said Edgar, holding on tight to the bridge and to his wife.

"I'm *terrified* of heights," said Shirley.

"You are?" said Cheyenne. "But you can't be—you're a spider."

"But remember, I wasn't always, dear," said Shirley. "I was terrified of heights while I was still human. Some things don't change. I'll be okay as long as I don't look down."

Although they were moving upward at a torturously slow pace, at last they were no more than ten feet from Dad. He had somehow freed himself from his upside-down position, but now he seemed weak and frightened.

"Dad!" Wally shouted. "Hang on! We'll save you!"

"I can't hold on much longer," said Dad. "I'm so glad you two aren't dead. If I have to let go, I just want you kids to know that it wasn't really okay with me for you to be adopted by the Spydelles. I was just following through on a promise I made if Cheyenne pulled through her fever."

"Really? I can't believe this!" said Cheyenne. "Dad, we want you to know that we never loved the Spydelles that much."

"What?" said Edgar.

"As much as we *love* the Spydelles," said Cheyenne, looking in Edgar's direction, "—and we *do* love them—we love you *more,* Dad."

"Then why did you say you wanted them to adopt you?" Dad asked.

"We were trying to save Edgar's life," said Wally. "Shirley wanted kids so badly, if we didn't get them to adopt us, she would have had a batch with Edgar—and then she'd have had to eat him."

Dad was crying now. "What a fool I've been," he said.

"We have *all* been fools," said Edgar. "Some bigger fools than others."

"But I'm the biggest fool of all," said Dad.

"No, my good fellow, I fear that honor goes to me," said Edgar.

"But I tried to drive a wooden stake through my heart that wasn't even wood, and I fired a silver bullet through my head that wasn't even real silver," said Dad.

"That *is* stupid, I grant you," said Edgar. "But I, on the other hand, am risking my bloody life climbing up a bloody bridge to rescue a bloody vampire who's determined to kill himself, and I'm doing it for two bloody children who said they wanted me to bloody adopt them but who, I now find out, hardly give a bloody fig about me."

"Oh, Edgar, that's not true," said Wally. "We do *so* give a bloody fig about you!"

"We give *lots* of bloody figs about you," said Cheyenne.

"Oh, right," said Edgar, turning his face away from them.

"Don't sulk, Edgar," said Shirley. "I will not have any sulking on this bridge."

"I really can't hold on anymore," said Dad.

"No! Hang on, Dad!" cried Wally. "We're almost up to you!"

"I can't, Wally. I've got cramps in both my hands," said Dad.

"Dad, what about your wings?" said Cheyenne. "Can't you just unfold your wings and float safely to the ground?"

"I already tried that," said Dad. "They're too cold. I can't unfurl them."

"Dad, please, just a couple more minutes and we'll be up to you!" said Cheyenne, stretching out an arm as far as it could reach, but finding it was at least seven feet short.

"I'm slipping," said Dad. "I just can't hold on anymore."

At these words, Dad's fingers lost their grip. He slipped another twenty feet, but grasping in panic at rusty iron cables, he somehow managed to grab hold of a cable and break his fall.

He was now about ten feet below them. In order to see him they had to look downward, and when they did, the incredibly long drop to the river below caused their breath to catch in their chests and made the skin on their scalps shrivel like prunes.

"Dad, are you all right?" called Cheyenne.

"Not really," he said. "I hurt my hands trying

142

to catch myself. I don't think I'll be able to hold on to this cable much longer."

"Then we have to do something quick to save you," said Wally. "Shirley, could you make some spider silk really fast?"

"Sure," said Shirley.

"Would it be strong enough to support the weight of three people?"

"Which three people?"

"Dad, Cheyenne, and me," said Wally.

"I think so," said Shirley. "You and Cheyenne don't weigh much at all. Even your dad is pretty skinny. And, for its size, spider silk is five times as strong as steel and twice as stretchy as nylon."

"Good," said Wally. "Then I have a plan to save Dad that just might work. Please squeeze out a piece of spider silk long enough for me and Cheyenne to wrap around ourselves. Then we're going to bungee-jump down to where Dad is."

"Oh, you want a dragline," said Shirley. "Why didn't you say so?"

Shirley grunted and, surprisingly fast, out of her abdomen came many coils of spider silk. It was clear and strong, like heavy nylon fisher-man's line. There was enough of it for Cheyenne and Wally to wrap it several times around their waists and still have lots left over.

"Hey, guys, my hands are really hurting!" Dad called. "I'm going to have to let go now. Good-bye. I love you."

"We're coming, Dad!" Wally yelled. "Just hang on a few seconds longer!"

"Hurry!" said Dad.

"Okay, Cheyenne," said Wally, "here comes the scary part. When I count to three, we're going to both let go of the bridge and let the spi-der silk break our fall. Then we're going to let Shirley guide the dragline over to Dad. Ready?"

"Ready," she answered.

"One . . . two . . . three!" said Wally.

Both twins let go of their hold on the bridge at the same moment.

"Whooooooaaaa!" they yelled.

They dropped so fast, it felt as if they were on a roller coaster, except that there was no reassuring roller coaster seat underneath them, just the yawning gorge.

When they had dropped thirty feet, they bounced back up again, just as if they really were attached to a bungee cord. Then they dropped again.

"Eeeeeeeeeeeeee!" they screamed.

As the bounces grew shorter and shorter, the wind began blowing them back and forth. It was a giddy and dizzying feeling to be that high up with nothing underneath them, and only a line of spider silk suspending them in space. Their stomachs were in their throats, their hearts in their mouths.

They were now twenty feet lower than Dad.

"Can you get any closer?" Dad called.

"Shirley!" Wally called. "Can you raise us up about twenty feet?"

"I'll try!"

Now they felt themselves being slowly hoisted higher. Three feet higher. Now five feet. Now seven. Now ten. Now thirteen.

The wind grew stronger and swung them back and forth in increasingly wider arcs. When they were almost even with Dad, Cheyenne and Wally stretched out both their arms, and Dad stretched out one of his. As the wind took them past Dad, he and Cheyenne brushed fingertips, but she couldn't grab him.

"Ohhhhhhhh!" she cried.

On their second pass, Wally almost got a grip on Dad's hand, but then he couldn't hold on to it.

"Darn!" said Wally.

On their third pass, both Cheyenne and

Wally actually got a grip on Dad—on his wrist, on his elbow, and on his nose.

"Got you!" screamed Cheyenne.

"Ouch!" said Dad.

"Sorry, Dad."

Dad let go of the bridge cable, wrapped his arms around both his children, and all three of them swung back into space.

"Thank you!" said Dad, tears filling his eyes.

"Shirley!" Wally yelled. "Can you lower us to the ground now?"

"I'll try!" she yelled back.

Slowly, slowly, with the wind taking them in wider and wider arcs that threatened to smash them into the bridge, Cheyenne, Wally, and Dad were lowered groundward on the spider silk dragline.

It took them five minutes to get all the way down, and when they did, all three fell to their knees and kissed the ground, as they'd seen people do on the TV news when they were rescued from an ordeal in the air.

"Ugh!" said Cheyenne, spitting out sand and dirt, "what a bad idea *that* was!"

"Yargh!" said Wally, wiping his lips and spitting, too, "why would anybody want to kiss the ground?"

"Shirley! Edgar!" Cheyenne shouted. "We made it! Come on down!"

# CHAPTER 21

# How Dare You Show Your Face?

"Your Highness," said a worker ont, bowing to the queen, "a visitor requests an urgent audience with you."

"Who makes such an impudent request?" asked the queen.

"A black-hat," said the worker.

"My time is occupied by my generals," said the queen. "I have no time for black-hats."

"It concerns the Shluffmuffin boy, Your Highness," said the worker.

"The Shluffmuffin boy?" The queen spat in disgust. "Very well, show her in."

A black-hatted figure, shorter than the others,

in sunglasses, cape, and full-length black gloves, was ushered into the queen's presence.

"Who demands an audience with Her Royal Highness?" the queen demanded.

In reply the visitor pulled off hat, sunglasses, and rubber mask.

"The Jackal," he said.

"So, you came," said the Ont Queen, biting off the end of a fresh cigar with a snap of her razor-sharp mandibles. "We didn't think you'd dare to show your face."

"You didn't think I'd dare to show *my* face?" said The Jackal. "The second fifty thousand was never deposited in the secret piggy bank in the locker at the Toledo bus station!"

"The Shluffmuffin boy is still alive," said the queen. She shook with fury.

"Alive?" said The Jackal. "That . . . that could not be. That simply isn't possible. I left him lying on the floor in an irreversible fatal coma caused by insulin shock."

"Well, somebody better tell that to Wally

Shluffmuffin," said Hedy Mandible, "because the poor devil thinks he's still alive."

"You have actually seen him alive?" asked The Jackal.

"Not me, dear," said Hedy, "but others have. He is *definitely* not dead. So if you're thinking of asking us for any letters of recommendation, I'd forget about it. And we'd like our fifty thousand back."

The stranger massaged his closed eyes with his paws.

"All right," he said. "Look, there has obviously been an unforeseen miscalculation. You have my deepest apologies. I am a professional. I stand behind my work. If you give me another chance, I promise you the Shluffmuffin boy will be roadkill by the end of the week. And to make up for my error, this time he will truly suffer. Will you give me another chance?"

"We shouldn't," said the queen, "but the babies are ravenous today, and we are feeling unusually generous. All right, you may have one week."

"I shall not fail you this time," said The Jackal.

"See that you don't," said the queen coldly.

CHAPTER 22

# The New Wally Isn't Worried

That night Wally and Cheyenne lay on their beds and talked long after the lights had been turned out. They listened to the *kreek*ing of the crickets in the forest and the mournful *arooooo* of a hungry wolf, and they discussed the exciting events of the day.

"You were great out there on the bridge," said Wally.

"You were even better," said Cheyenne. "And what about Shirley—was she fantastic or what?"

"She was awesome," said Wally. "And I'm so glad we cleared up all the misunderstandings with Dad. It's too bad that Edgar's sulking now, but I'm sure he'll get over it." Wally stopped and took a deep breath. "Cheyenne, you're not going to love hearing this, but I have to tell you, anyway."

"What?"

"You know the guy from the Centers for Disease Control who gave me that messed-up shot? It was an overdose of insulin strong enough to kill me."

"You're sure of that?" she said.

"Oh yeah, I'm sure all right," he said. "If I hadn't had that Choco-Doodle-Doo bar with me, I'd be dead by now. The amount of sugar I had in my bloodstream must have been just enough to counteract all that insulin and save my life. But somebody is definitely out to kill me."

"But, Wally, who'd want to kill you?"

"The Ont Queen," he said. "Or one of her buddies. You know where I went before I got that injection? Back to snoop around the Ont Queen's cave. Wait till I tell you what I found out. I actually heard her telling someone what she plans to do to the human race. Cheyenne, you, me, Edgar, Shirley, and Dad are the only ones who can save us from being enslaved by giant onts that are determined to end life on Earth as we know it! Are you with me on this?"

"Of course I am, silly," she said. "We beat the onts before, and we can do it again. Shluff-muffins rule!"

# What's Next for the Shluffmuffin Twins?

Now that Edgar Spydelle has heard Cheyenne and Wally say they love Vampire Dad better than him, is he going to sulk and be a total pain in the butt about it? If he does, how will that reduce his effectiveness as a team member against the onts?

Now that Shirley has heard that she and Edgar won't be adopting the twins after all, how long will it be before she insists that she and Edgar mate, thus forcing her to kill him and eat him?

Now that Vampire Dad knows the twins want to live with him, do you think he'll be able to find them all a place to live and get a job so he can pay for rent and food? How easy do you think it will be for a dead person with fangs and wings and an unquenchable thirst for human blood to convince somebody to rent him an apartment— or to give him a job?

If Dad is going to live with the twins, that means Hortense Jolly won't be able to get anyone to pay her outrageous adoption fee. Will she take this news calmly and graciously, or will she do something spiteful and vengeful that will get our friends in terrible trouble?

What hideous new plan will The Jackal concoct to try to kill poor Wally? Will the frustration and humiliation he suffered at failing to kill Wally the first time cause him to come up with an even crueler death than an insulin overdose? If so, how can a ten-year-old boy, even a *resourceful* ten-year-old boy who has practically memorized the entire encyclopedia, possibly hope to survive against a professional assassin—even one who happens to be a good deal furrier than most?

Well, unless The Jackal figures out a way to have Wally attacked by something as unlikely as, oh, let's say, a giant octopus, he'll probably be okay. (Uh-oh, we just found out that Secrets of Dripping Fang, Book Six is called *Attack of the Giant Octopus*!)

Finally, what of the Ont Queen and her army of soldiers? How long will it be before they begin their evil plan to enslave humans and end life on Earth as we know it? Do you think that just because they're in a book and you're not that you'll be safe from them? If so, what's that noise coming from the kitchen—that soft scratching at the screen door? You didn't hear it? Listen. There it is again. Oh well, it's probably nothing. . . .

DAN GREENBURG writes the popular Zack Files series for kids and has also written many bestselling books for grown-ups. His seventy books have been translated into twenty languages. To research his writing, Dan has worked with N.Y. firefighters and homicide cops, searched for the Loch Ness monster, flown upside down in an open-cockpit plane, taken part in voodoo ceremonies in Haiti, and disciplined tigers on a Texas ranch. He has not, however, personally encountered any zombies or vampires—at least not yet. Dan lives north of New York with wife Judith, son Zack, and many cats.

SCOTT M. FISCHER glided through high school doing extra-credit art assignments for math teachers, which is kinda boring stuff to draw. Next he went to art school, where he learned to paint even more boring things—like flower vases. However, he swears that since then he has drawn nothing but cool stuff—like oozy, drooling monsters, treacherous villains, and the occasional flower vase . . . that has fangs and eats flowers for breakfast!